In the Paths of Righteousness

Other Books by Debbie Viguié

<u>The Psalm 23 Mysteries</u>

The Lord is My Shepherd
I Shall Not Want
Lie Down in Green Pastures
Beside Still Waters
Restoreth My Soul

<u>The Kiss Trilogy</u>

Kiss of Night
Kiss of Death
Kiss of Revenge

<u>Sweet Seasons</u>

The Summer of Cotton Candy
The Fall of Candy Corn
The Winter of Candy Canes
The Spring of Candy Apples

<u>Witch Hunt</u>

The Thirteenth Sacrifice
The Last Grave

In the Paths of Righteousness

Psalm 23 Mysteries

By Debbie Viguié

Published by Big Pink Bow

In the Paths of Righteousness

ISBN-13: 978-0615860268

Published by Big Pink Bow

www.bigpinkbow.com

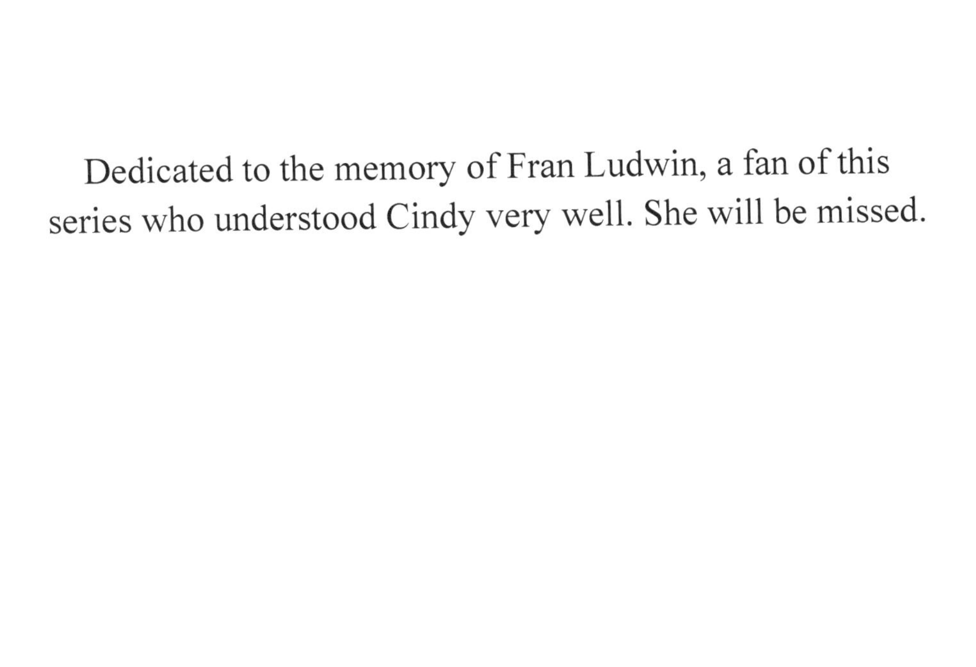

Dedicated to the memory of Fran Ludwin, a fan of this series who understood Cindy very well. She will be missed.

Thank you to everyone who helped make this book a reality, particularly Barbara Reynolds, Rick Reynolds and Calliope Collacott. A special thank you to my Superfans: Melanie Smith, Karen Cruz, Angie Arey, Becky Lewis, Michelle Flint, Tina Grinde and Jennifer Roland. Without you guys this book wouldn't exist. Thank you for your continued support.

1

Jeremiah Silverman usually loved Sundays. They were one of his days off and always a welcome respite after spending the Sabbath working at the synagogue. It was always ironic. The Sabbath wasn't supposed to be about work, but as a rabbi, it was kind of unavoidable. So, while Saturday was the Sabbath, Sunday was usually his day of rest.

Only, not this Sunday. This Sunday was one of the more stressful he'd spent in a while. And for once it wasn't because he was dealing with a dead body. No, the person causing him such great distress was living and breathing. And no matter how much Jeremiah wished that he could change that, he really couldn't. Well, he really *shouldn't.*

The truth was he'd spent all of ten minutes in the presence of Kyle Preston and he could already tell that it was going to be an incredibly long week. If both of them survived it would be nothing short of a miracle.

Kyle Preston was a travel show host for the Escape! Channel. He specialized in all the crazy, insane things that so many people dreamed about and only insane people actually did. He was exuberant, arrogant, and, most importantly, Cindy's brother.

Jeremiah glanced over at Cindy Preston. Cindy was the secretary at the church next door to his synagogue. More than that she was his friend. His best friend if he was being honest with himself. More honest than that he tried to avoid being.

Cindy was looking incredibly flustered and he knew that it had to be hard to have her worlds colliding. After all, it was the first time any one of her family members had met her friends. Worse, it was happening on Kyle's terms and not hers.

"I blame you for all of this," Mark whispered under his breath from where he sat next to Jeremiah on a bale of hay. The detective was clearly not happy.

"It's going to be fun," Traci, Mark's wife, said brightly from his other side.

Fun.

Jeremiah took a deep breath. His idea of fun was going to The Zone theme park or the movies or just hanging out with Cindy and talking about things that didn't even matter. Wilderness treks were not his idea of fun. They were too much a reminder of times in his own past he'd rather forget. But for Cindy's sake he plastered a smile on his face. He would try to get along with Kyle, too. After all, the guy actually thought he was doing something nice for the rest of them.

"This is going to be the best vacation any of you have ever had," Kyle enthused, wrapping up his welcome speech.

"You didn't say anything about us being followed around by television cameras," Mark said.

It was true. Cindy had been kidnapped a few months before and Mark and Jeremiah had both been instrumental in her rescue. As a thank you Kyle had decided to use his connections to take them all with him on a week-long cattle drive vacation. He had insisted that Cindy come and bring Jeremiah, Mark, and Traci along with her. Traci was the only one who had been excited about the prospect, not because she wanted to spend a week on horseback driving a herd of cattle but because she was a huge fan of Kyle's. Jeremiah didn't envy Mark the headache of keeping his wife's enthusiasm in check.

Of course, Jeremiah was far more worried about the television cameras than anything else. He had thought about leaving the moment he found out, but that would mean explaining a lot to Cindy that he wasn't ready to do just yet. Camera shy didn't begin to cover his problem. With a sigh he decided that the best solution was just to try and get through the week and then make sure the footage was destroyed before it could ever see the light of day.

"Alright, chow's on!" Kyle said excitedly.

They all stood up and filed over to the chuck wagon where tin bowls waited them. The camp cook heaped them full of stew and Jeremiah looked at his bowl distrustfully. Kyle walked up and clapped a hand on his shoulder. "Don't worry, we may be doing this whole trip authentic style, totally roughing it, but I told them all the food had to be kosher. The chef even found a recipe to make bacon out of lamb, so hopefully it will all be amazing."

Jeremiah forced himself to smile. "Thanks," he said.

"Of course," Kyle said cheerfully.

He really is trying to be nice, Jeremiah reminded himself, even though he found the man off-putting. Of course, that could have something to do with the fact that he knew that Cindy had a dartboard with her brother's face on it that she routinely used as target practice.

They all headed back to their bales of hay with full bowls and sat down. They had arrived less than an hour before, having to take a helicopter to reach the spot where they were now which was in the middle of nowhere. There was a rundown cabin behind them, the chuck wagon, and a corral filled with horses. Kyle's crew who would be accompanying them, consisted of half a dozen people who were huddled together on another set of hay bales several feet away. The three professional cowboys were also keeping to themselves. Counting the cook it was going to be a group of fifteen heading out in the morning.

Kyle's producer and an older gentleman who apparently was co-owner of the adventure tour they were going on would be taking the helicopter back in the morning. For the rest of them, there would be no civilization for six days, just miles of open range and sore rumps. They would be sleeping under the stars so Kyle had encouraged all of them to pray for good weather.

"I'm sorry I got you all into this," Cindy said as she perched with her bowl on her knees.

Traci smiled at her brightly. "Are you kidding? This is going to be the best vacation ever! Nobody could believe it when I told them I was going on a trip with Kyle Preston."

Mark rolled his eyes.

Cindy grinned and the sight lifted Jeremiah's spirits. He had been taken aback by the camera crew and he had to admit he had been prepared to dislike Kyle. The truth was, though, anywhere with Cindy was better than anywhere else without her.

"Sure, it's going to be a lot of fun," Jeremiah said. "It's been a couple of years since I've been on a horse, so it will be good to ride again. And being out in nature is always a good thing, makes it easy to commune with G-d and spend time laughing with the people you care about."

Mark looked like he was about to say something sarcastic, but Cindy jumped in. "I've never ridden a horse," she confessed.

"Me either," Mark said.

Jeremiah winced. The two of them were in for a rude awakening and were going to be incredibly sore for most of the journey.

"I took lessons when I was a kid," Traci said. "I always dreamed of riding in the Olympics. You want to hear something funny? I've never actually ridden a Western saddle before, though."

"There's more to hang on to," Jeremiah said.

"Lucky for us," Cindy added. She looked nervous, though.

He hadn't thought about it before, but this had to be way out of her comfort zone, especially if she'd never ridden at all. It was logical that she'd be nervous, especially given how risk adverse she was. Of course, even that seemed to be changing more every day. He figured that was a natural side effect of all the mysteries they'd solved together in the last year-and-a-half, all the dangerous situations she'd been in.

He reached over and squeezed her hand. "You're going to be fine," he reassured her. "I won't let anything bad happen to you." He held her hand for a few moments longer than necessary, loathe to let go. He finally forced himself to with an inward sigh. She turned her head and a strand of her light brown hair fell across her face. He barely resisted the urge to tuck it behind her ear. The relationship with her was getting more complicated and he didn't know what to do about it.

"So, what is the deal with your brother?" Mark asked.

They all turned to look at Kyle. He was tall, tan, and blonde. He was wearing clothes that in style and color were a cross between cowboy gear and adventurer wear. He bounced lightly on the balls of his feet as he moved, as though he was filled with energy that was just dying to burst forth at any moment. In addition to the energy he had a lot of charisma, the perfect combination for the host of a television travel show. He was a minor celebrity, and Jeremiah knew that Cindy's parents favored her brother which drove her crazy.

"He's been a daredevil since we were kids," Cindy said, sounding far away. "I used to get so mad at him because I felt like he was taking foolish risks with his life."

"Used to be?" Traci asked.

Cindy turned back and shrugged. "I guess if I've learned anything the last year or so it's that risk is everywhere and it doesn't matter how safe you try to be, sometimes danger finds you."

"True enough," Mark muttered.

"Okay, everyone, head inside and grab your bunk. We'll need to get a good night's rest because we're starting out fresh in the morning," Kyle addressed everyone.

Jeremiah gazed around the little group. The truth was the last year had brought a lot of trauma to all of them and changed their lives in profound ways. "You know, if ever four people needed a vacation," he said slowly, "it's us."

Traci grinned and nodded her head. "Agreed, and I, for one, plan to squeeze all the enjoyment I can out of this week. Who knows what the future holds, when we will all get a chance to just relax and hang out together. I think this might just be the best vacation ever."

"Famous last words," Mark quipped as they stood inside the ramshackle cabin and surveyed their bunks.

Cindy shook her head. "I'm glad I brought my own pillow case."

"You were smart," Traci groaned.

"Paranoid is what I thought I was," Cindy admitted.

The sheets piled on top of each bunk were light gray and she wasn't sure if that was on purpose.

"Flashbacks to summer camp hell," Mark muttered. Then she saw him wince and glance at Jeremiah. "Sorry."

Jeremiah just shook his head.

"At least it's just for one night," Cindy said, struggling to hold on to the cheerfulness she'd felt just a few minutes before.

Jeremiah moved to claim a top bunk on the far side of the cabin. Cindy started to pick the one below him, but he shook his head and signaled to the top bunk next to his. "Farther off the floor is better," he said, although he didn't explain what he meant by that.

She wrinkled her nose, wondering if they could expect any furry visitors in the night. She hoped not. She quickly worked to make up her bunk and when she was finished she realized that she and Jeremiah would be sleeping with their heads just inches apart. For some reason the thought made her blush and she turned away from him to hide it. She caught Traci grinning at her and she resisted the urge to throw her pillow at her. She didn't want her clean pillow case anywhere near the floor.

"Pillow fight later?" Mark joked, as though reading her mind.

Traci rolled her eyes. "Sure, it's all fun and games until someone forgets to take their flashlight out of their pillowcase before it starts."

"Ouch!" Cindy said. "Please tell me that didn't happen to you."

"I'm afraid it did," Traci said.

"Were you the hitter or the hittee?"

"Both."

Behind her Cindy could swear she heard Jeremiah stifle a chuckle.

Besides her and Traci there was one other woman in the group, a makeup artist named Liz. Cindy couldn't even begin to fathom how Kyle thought he was going to need a makeup person when he was trailing through the dust every day. She was grateful, though, that one of his crew was female. They were still vastly outnumbered, but three was better than two.

Kyle came into the cabin. "I want to thank you all for joining me on this journey. We're riding into the unknown and it will test our limits, but I believe that is the highest goal a man can attain. I chose Columbus Day to start our journey because I believe that like his voyage across the sea, this will be a journey of discovery for each of us. We might not be discovering a new land, but we could be discovering new friends, new depths of strength and courage, and things about ourselves we might never otherwise have known. I see this as the beginning of a great adventure and I'm proud to be embarking on it with all of you."

His crew broke into applause and after a moment Cindy joined in half-heartedly. She most certainly didn't want to learn anything new about herself on this journey. She was still struggling to come to grips with everything that had happened to her and she was still struggling with the PTSD that had been plaguing her for the last several weeks. However, she did wish wistfully that the trip might bring her and Kyle closer together so that part she could definitely get behind.

"Alright everyone, that's it. Lights out in twenty minutes," he said.

There was a sudden flurry of activity as people moved toward the bathroom that was in the back of the cabin. Liz got there first and she turned around barring the way. "Girls first!" she said firmly.

A couple of guys groused but they turned away. Cindy hurriedly grabbed her bag and she and Traci ran over to join Liz.

"We girls have to stick together," Liz said under her breath.

"I couldn't agree more," Cindy whispered back.

The tile in the bathroom was slippery and Cindy slid slightly after taking off her shoes. "Careful, it's slick," she said.

"I noticed, I almost did my best Bambi impression," Traci said.

Ten minutes later Cindy was back in the main cabin wearing her fleecy pajamas, the ones with cats on them. Kyle had warned her that the nights could get cold, but she would have chosen the pajamas anyway since she was going to be spending the week in mixed company. She noticed that the other two women had made similar choices, although less whimsical than hers.

Jeremiah looked at her and smiled.

"What?"

"Nothing. You look very...cozy."

"I am," she said, smiling.

She hoisted herself up onto her bunk and prepared to lay down. She tucked her flashlight under her pillow and bit back a laugh when she saw Traci putting hers inside her pillow case. Traci caught her smiling and shrugged. "Old habits die hard."

Mark and Jeremiah headed toward the restrooms with everyone else. They were both back quickly. A couple of minutes later everyone was in bed and someone turned off the lights.

Cindy lay still in the dark, her heart pounding, hyper aware of just how close Jeremiah was.

"Shouldn't someone tell a ghost story?" Traci whispered.

Someone else tried to shush her and Cindy fought back a hysterical case of the giggles. She failed and flipped over, trying to at least laugh into her pillow. She heard a couple of others join in.

"This is why girls and boys should have separate cabins. The boys want to sleep," she heard one guy sigh.

For some reason it just struck her as funny and she started laughing harder.

A moment later Jeremiah whispered, "What kind of ghost story?"

"I will hurt you," she heard Mark threaten.

All the stress and anxiety that she had carried with her for so long just spilled over and Cindy began shaking with the laughter she couldn't contain.

"Come on guys," she heard Kyle say, sounding so much like their father that it just sent her into further fits.

It took twenty minutes and two failed attempts at ghost stories before they all began to fall asleep. Cindy drowsed at the last, feeling more at peace than she had in a long time. It didn't make any sense, but there it was. She was beginning to think maybe this would be the best vacation ever. Heaven knew she needed one, a real one.

She heard Jeremiah's breathing slow down even further and she was sure he must have finally fallen asleep. She lay there for what seemed a long time listening to the sounds of the night. People began to snore and she smiled but managed not to start laughing again. Beds creaked as their occupants moved around. Outside she could hear crickets. She could feel herself finally getting drowsy. She flipped onto her side, started to pray, and fell asleep before she could finish.

A piercing scream caused her to sit bolt upright. She grabbed for her flashlight and switched it on. A moment later several others came on as well. She hit the floor, the thud incredibly loud in the silence following the scream. She winced slightly at the impact on her ankles.

"What was that?" she asked.

"It came from the bathroom," Jeremiah said. He was standing next to her and she hadn't even heard him hit the ground.

"Where's Traci?" Mark demanded a moment later. Cindy shone her light toward the other woman's bunk and saw that she wasn't there.

Heart in her throat, Cindy ran toward the bathroom, her light bobbing all over. She had no idea where the light switches were and no time to waste looking for them.

She skidded into the bathroom and saw Traci standing, clutching a sink. She had one hand clamped over her mouth and she was staring downward, eyes wide in horror.

Cindy dropped the beam of her light toward Traci's feet. There on the floor was the body of a man, blood pooling underneath his head.

2

Thank heavens I wasn't the one who found him, Cindy thought to herself as she stood, flashlight trained on the dead man. A moment later lights flooded on behind her in the cabin. She felt a hand on her shoulder and glanced back to see Jeremiah standing behind her. He reached over and found the light switch in the bathroom and turned it on.

Mark entered the room a moment later and reached for Traci who leaped over the body and flew into his arms, sliding slightly in the blood on the floor.

Kyle burst into the room, his hair sticking straight up, wearing grey sweats and an old Star Wars T-shirt that seemed vaguely familiar to her and was way too small for him.

"What happened?" he asked.

She pointed to the floor and he dropped his eyes. "Martin!" he shouted and started to drop to his knees.

Cindy grabbed him and pulled him back. "Don't touch the body," she hissed.

"Body?" he asked, sounding dazed. "That's Martin. We have to help him."

"We can't help him. He's dead."

He turned and stared at her, eyes large and glassy looking. "That's not possible," he whispered after a moment.

"I'm afraid it is," she said, putting her arms around him and hugging him.

He just stood there, unmoving, and her heart ached for him. She remembered how it had felt when she'd tripped over the dead body in the sanctuary, and she hadn't even known that guy.

"Take him in the other room," Jeremiah said softly.

She nodded. She pulled away from Kyle and took his arm. He didn't fight her as she led him back into the main cabin, but he kept staring back over his shoulder. She forced him to sit down on one of the lower bunks, she thought it was Mark's. Then she sat beside him and put her arm around him.

"It's going to be okay," she told him quietly.

"Martin's dead," he said numbly.

She nodded. He had introduced all his crew when everyone had arrived and she was struggling to remember what he'd said Martin's job was. She was pretty sure he was the cameraman. She could be wrong, though. As she rubbed his shoulder she couldn't help but notice that the T-shirt was full of holes and well worn. It had seen far too many washings and she wondered idly given how small it was why he didn't just throw it out.

A few minutes later Mark was sitting Traci down on Cindy's other side. She put an arm around her as well and just sat, trying to offer what comfort she could to both of them.

It seemed to take forever but police finally arrived and took charge of the scene. Soon everyone was in the main cabin area sitting on bunks, including Jeremiah. Mark was the only one who was still in the bathroom area talking with the officers.

"I didn't want to turn on my flashlight," Traci said woodenly.

Cindy turned to look at her. "What?" she asked.

"I didn't want to wake anyone up and there was just enough light coming through the window that I thought I could just get up and go to the bathroom and it would be okay. Then I kicked something and fell against the sink."

"And that's when you screamed," Cindy said.

"Did I? I don't remember," Traci said, sounding dazed.

"You did. That's what woke me up," Cindy told her.

"It woke everyone up," Kyle said.

"I'm sorry," Traci said.

It was a ridiculous thing to apologize for, but Cindy could tell that Traci was in shock. Kyle was, too. She thought it spoke volumes that she, herself, felt fine. When had dead bodies become commonplace?

"Are you okay?" Jeremiah asked.

Cindy nodded. "I think we could use some blankets and maybe some tea or apple juice or something for these two."

She had been learning recently that apple juice did wonders to calm her down when she was starting to freak out.

"I've got tea I can make," the cook volunteered.

"Mark," Cindy called.

The detective entered the room and came quickly over. "What is it?" he asked, looking worriedly at his wife.

"The cook volunteered to make some tea for those who need it," Cindy said.

Mark nodded. "That should be fine. I'll let the sheriff know."

The cook got up and headed outside to the chuck wagon. He returned a few minutes later with some steaming mugs which he handed to Kyle and Traci. Traci took hers and then looked up at him. "I know you," she said.

He nodded grimly. "Yeah, when the bosses at the Escape! Channel suggested this to me I thought it might be kind of fun. I'm rethinking that at the moment." He straightened up and looked around. "Who else needs tea?"

A couple of others raised their hands and he left to get more mugs.

"Who is he?" Cindy asked, struggling to remember how her brother had introduced him. She was pretty sure it had just been a fake, old west kind of name like Cookie.

"Brent Joelson. He's a famous chef, owns a bunch of really high-end restaurants."

Cindy blinked. "And he agreed to be our camp cook?"

"It seemed like a good idea," Kyle muttered after taking a sip of his tea. "The network wanted to see how long before viewers figured out who he was. They wanted to have a few different Escape! Channel hosts show up. Bunni Sinclair was supposed to come, but she broke her leg while filming an updated segment for Girl Meets Guam."

Traci winced. "I always feel so sorry for her. Terrible things always seem to happen to her."

Cindy could relate, but she didn't say so.

Detective Mark Walters wondered if he was the cursed one or if it was Cindy. After a moment's thought he decided it had to be Cindy. He just had the misfortune of being here as did Traci. He winced, feeling incredibly bad for his wife. She had been so excited about the trip, too, that it just made him feel guilty that he'd been such a jerk about it. He'd find a way to make it up to her.

After the year they'd had, they both deserved something nice. Maybe a second honeymoon somewhere. He began to warm to the thought even as he stood in the cold bathroom waiting to see if the sheriff needed anything more from him.

On the plus side it looked like the dead man had just fallen on the slippery tile, hit his head on a sink, and died. It was tragic, but a matter for the lawyers and insurance companies, not for homicide detectives. Which was a relief to say the least. He got enough of murder and mayhem at home without dealing with it on vacation.

"I don't see anything to make me think this wasn't just an accident," the sheriff said at last.

Mark nodded.

"Still, I'll need to take statements from everyone else, just in case," the man said with a sigh.

Mark could feel his pain. It was the middle of the night and both of them wanted nothing more than to get some sleep. Mark led him into the other room.

"Everyone, this is Sheriff Danvers," Mark said, feeling the need to make an introduction.

"Thank you, Detective. I'd like everyone to just sit tight. I've got to ask a few questions, but I'll try to be as quick as possible."

Around the room heads bobbed up and down. Fear mixed with grief on several faces. For most this was probably the first dead body they'd encountered, at least, like this.

"Is there anything you need me to do, Sheriff?" he asked.

"I'll let you know if I think of anything."

Mark headed over and just managed to squeeze into the space on the other side of Traci. Cindy was still wedged in between her and Kyle. Jeremiah was standing, leaning against a bunk, arms folded across his chest, attempting to look casual. But Mark could see the way his eyes were roving over everything and everyone. He was clearly worried, and given their history he had good reason to be.

"Don't worry," he said quietly to Cindy, but loud enough that he knew Jeremiah would hear. "It looks like it was just an unfortunate accident."

Cindy looked relieved. Jeremiah flicked his eyes toward Mark's briefly and he could tell the rabbi wasn't convinced.

Traci was looking better than she had before and she had almost finished drinking her tea. He put his arm around her and hugged her tight and she leaned her head on his shoulder.

"I'm so sorry," he whispered.

"It's not your fault."

Jeremiah watched as the sheriff made the rounds, asking people the same few questions. Everyone had the same answers. No one had seen or heard anything until Traci screamed. No one knew of any problems that Martin had. It was all very predictable.

Jeremiah had gotten a good look at the accident scene. Mark was right. It looked like a classic slip and fall accident. The floor was slick enough that it was inevitable that someone would fall on it. Hitting his head on the sink had been the tragic part.

Still, Jeremiah couldn't shake the feeling that it wasn't an accident. He tried to tell himself that he was being paranoid. There was nothing to suggest that it was anything but an accident. He had been sound asleep until Traci screamed and he hadn't heard or seen anything suspicious before. Everyone in the cabin seemed genuinely shocked.

When the sheriff finished questioning everyone it was nearly two in the morning. The general consensus was that no one wanted to go back to sleep in the cabin so close to the spot where Martin had died. The sleeping blankets that they would have been using on the trail were broken out as everyone moved outside. It was cold, but the sleeping bags were warm and everyone was exhausted.

Within minutes people began to fall asleep until Jeremiah was the last one awake. He was still feeling unsettled and when he finally did go to sleep, he slept lightly, prepared to rise at the slightest hint that anything was wrong.

Cindy could hear the sounds of people getting up and moving around. She could tell that it was light out, but she wasn't ready to get up yet. She laid still, snuggled inside her sleeping blanket. Her hand was wrapped around her flashlight just as it had been when she had finally fallen asleep.

At the time she had told herself it was just because she was worried about finding it easily if she needed to get up for anything. In truth, though, she realized she'd been worried something else would happen in the middle of the night.

Those fears seemed silly now, though. It had been an accident. That's what the sheriff and Mark both had said. Somehow in the light of morning it was easier to believe.

Suddenly she smelled bacon and that proved to be too much of a temptation. She opened her eyes slowly and looked around. Next to her Traci was just starting to sit up. Jeremiah, Mark, and Kyle's sleeping bags were all empty. Several people were standing around in various states of waking.

She reached over and touched Traci's shoulder. "How are you feeling?"

"Better. Not good, but better. And hungry, surprisingly. I think I could eat everyone's share of bacon by myself."

Cindy grinned. "I'll take that as a good sign."

Traci frowned. "Unfortunately, before I eat anything I need to use the restroom."

"I've been wondering for the last minute or so how to avoid that myself," Cindy admitted.

"Mark told me about that first day you met. How did you force yourself to go back into the sanctuary after you tripped over that body there?"

"It was either force myself to deal with it or get a new job. In the end dealing seemed the better choice," Cindy said.

"Okay. So, come help me deal with this?"

"You bet."

When they made it into the bathroom Cindy was relieved to see that someone had already cleaned up and gotten rid of the blood. Still Traci and she both gave the spot a wide berth and hurried to finish changing and get out of there.

She breathed easier once they were back outside. They found Jeremiah and Mark standing together a little ways away from everyone else. Cindy's stomach rumbled loudly as the smell of bacon became nearly overpowering.

"What's going on?" she asked.

"A couple of new people arrived this morning. I think one of them is Kyle's boss. Not sure who the other one is."

"When do you think they're going to bring in the helicopter to pick us up?" Cindy asked.

Mark shrugged. "It's hard to say."

"While we wait to see what's going on we might as well eat," Jeremiah said just as Cindy's stomach rumbled again.

She realized she hadn't eaten much of the stew the night before. She had been nervous enough she hadn't really tasted anything. It was a shame. How often did she have a chance to eat food prepared by a famous chef?

Breakfast was pretty standard fare including bacon, eggs, and biscuits. It was all delicious, though.

Everyone ate in the same small groups that they had the night before but this time it was much quieter, the mood definitely subdued. It was a stark contrast to the night before and Cindy couldn't help but feel a little sad, especially when she looked at Traci. The other woman's enthusiasm had started rubbing off on her and now she felt a little lost at the thought that they weren't going to get to even start on their journey let alone complete it.

She noticed that Kyle seemed a lot better than he had the night before. He was standing apart from everyone having an animated conversation with the man she guessed was his boss. She couldn't help but wonder how the whole mess was going to affect his new show.

As soon as they had finished eating they all packed up their gear. It took Cindy three tries to roll her sleeping bag up as tightly as it had been before. Jeremiah offered to help after he finished packing his stuff but she felt the need to accomplish it herself. When she had she felt a small amount of pride and he just grinned at her. Whenever he smiled like that it made her feel warm inside.

When they were all packed up they ended up sitting back on the same hay bales they had sat on for dinner and breakfast. She could see the corral with the horses and she noticed that the cowboys were busy saddling them up.

"Look," she said, pointing. "What do you think is going on?" she asked.

"That's an excellent question," Jeremiah muttered.

She turned to look for her brother and saw him making the rounds of his crew. He had a smile plastered across his face that only looked a little strained and he was shaking hands one after the other. He would know what was going on and when they were getting out of there if anyone would.

"I'll be right back," she said to the others and walked over to Kyle.

He saw her and finished shaking Liz's hand and walked to meet her.

"How are you holding up?" she asked him.

"I've been better, but I've also been a lot worse," he said, no longer smiling.

"Yeah, me, too," she said with a shiver.

For a moment it hung in the air between them, the memory of what had happened to their sister. She could tell they were both thinking about it, but neither of them wanted to say anything. Impulsively she reached out and hugged him. He hugged her back for a moment before pulling away.

"So, when is the helicopter coming to take us home?" she asked after a moment.

The smile returned to his face. "Yeah, about that. I'll be making an announcement in a couple of minutes."

"Can't you just tell me now?"

"Best to wait. It won't be but a minute or two," he said.

Irritated she nodded and headed back over to rejoin the others.

"He says he'll make an announcement in a few minutes."

"I hope he hurries," Mark said with a sigh.

Cindy returned her attention to the horses and was surprised to see that they were now all saddled and standing in a line with their reins tied to the fence. A sudden suspicion formed in her mind, but she told herself she had to be wrong.

A minute later Kyle jumped up onto a bale of hay. He stood there, smile planted firmly in place, beaming at everyone. He was larger than life.

"First off, I'd like to say thank you to everyone for how well you've been hanging in there. I know it was a rough night for everyone. I wanted to introduce you to a couple of new faces." Kyle gestured to a tall Native American man who had a thick black braid that hung down his back. "This is Hank Lightfoot."

Hank nodded solemnly.

"And over here," he said, gesturing to a short man with pasty white skin and thick, round glasses, "is Norman Smith."

Norman gave a short, nervous wave to everyone.

"They're going to be joining us from here on out and I want you to welcome them aboard."

There was a scattering of applause as Cindy blinked in surprise. "Excuse me," she said, standing up after a moment.

Kyle turned to look at her. "Yes?" he asked, raising one eyebrow.

"What do you mean 'joining us'?"

Kyle nodded. "Aaron left this morning after what happened. That left us two men short. Hence joining."

"You mean, you still plan to go through with this?" Mark piped up.

"Of course. It was an accident, a terrible, tragic accident, but we all have jobs to do. And everyone here understands the same thing that Martin did."

"And just what is that?" Cindy asked.

Kyle's smile only got bigger. "The show must go on."

3

Jeremiah had been fairly certain this was coming. He hadn't told the others, though, because that would have meant admitting that he could read lips and from quite a distance. He had been watching as Kyle talked to his producer and that was how he knew Hank and Norman were replacement crew. The only thing that surprised him was just how fast the network had managed to get them there.

"He can't be serious," he heard Mark say.

"I'm pretty sure he is," Jeremiah answered quietly.

He glanced at Cindy to see how she was reacting. She looked angry.

Kyle continued. "Everyone on horseback except our cowboys will be wearing protective helmets. This gives us the added advantage of being able to add cameras so that we can see what you're seeing."

He held up a helmet. "You just switch it on like this," he said, demonstrating. "Simple."

"I'm going to kill him," Cindy breathed.

Jeremiah was right there with her. That was several more cameras to sabotage. It was a lot of effort to make sure that his face would never show up on television. He took a deep breath. Maybe it wasn't too late to get out of all of this. It would be easier.

"I can't believe he's not sending us home or at least postponing," Mark said, "some people have had a great deal of trauma."

It was clear that Mark was referencing his wife, but there were those on the crew who had probably known Martin and would need space to deal with their grief over his death.

Traci paled noticeably and Jeremiah couldn't help but feel sorry for her.

Mark had just about had enough. Enough blood. Enough surprises. Enough tragedy striking in the vicinity of his wife. Enough...everything. It had been a brutal year, the worst one of his life. Traci was the only thing that had gotten him through all the terribleness, all the hard times.

He just wished he could protect her from the evil of the world, but it seemed like more and more he was bringing his work home with him. It wasn't right. To be honest, he wouldn't blame her for leaving. She hadn't yet, though. She just kept sticking by him and smiling despite all the hell he brought into her life.

Despite what had happened to Paul and what he himself had done to the suspect he was interrogating the day Paul died. He still had nightmares. Months to heal, extensive work ordered therapy, and with Jeremiah no less, hadn't managed to put an end to those. It had slowed them down, though. He had finally come to accept himself, accept how he'd tortured that suspect.

He hadn't come to accept that the man he had called partner for years had been living a lie. His partner Paul hadn't been who he said he was. The irony was, the body of the real Paul Dryer, killed as a child, had surfaced not that far away from where the fake Paul had died.

Since discovering that his partner's identity was a lie he had worked to discover the truth. He had combed old databases of missing kids hoping to discover who the fake Paul had been before assuming the identity of the Dryer family's kidnapped child. What made it even worse was that he seemed to be the only one who even cared. Paul's parents didn't want to accept the truth. Their money and influence had guaranteed that the police department didn't pursue the investigation. After all, both Pauls were dead. Only Paul's sister had given him any help, telling him that she had been suspicious that the boy who had come home a couple of years after being kidnapped wasn't her brother.

Since his search had been on his own time and not the department's, it had meant a lot of late nights. Traci hadn't complained once. She had even told him that she needed to know the truth as much as he did. He wasn't sure that was the case, but he was grateful for her support. He didn't deserve to be so lucky.

He should have taken her to Hawaii. This was a lousy way to spend a vacation. Truth be told, just being around Cindy and Jeremiah anymore made him think of death. At the rate they were helping to solve crimes both of them should have been on the police force. He smiled grimly, trying to imagine the chaos that would cause.

Cindy stared at Mark, wondering why he was smiling so oddly at her. She could tell he had thought of something that amused him although for the life of her she couldn't imagine what. She did know that he wanted to leave and head back home as much as she did.

"We should go," she said. "This whole thing was a bad idea. I'm sorry I let my crazy brother rope me into this and drag you along with me."

Traci reached out and laid a hand on her arm.

"Please. Let's not let last night ruin our vacation," Traci pleaded. "It's terrible, but if he'd had a heart attack or something during dinner I'm sure we wouldn't even be questioning going. I think it's just the way...the way I found him."

"She's right," Jeremiah said quietly. "For all we know Martin didn't even slip in the bathroom. He could have had a heart attack and fallen."

"I guess we should be grateful it happened here before the ride started instead of out there on the trail," Mark conceded.

Traitors. They were both clearly moved by Traci's desire to soldier on despite what had happened.

All eyes swiveled to Cindy. She didn't want to go, but then, that was nothing new. She was afraid of getting up on a horse and wasn't looking forward to being stuck in the middle of nowhere on one. However, if she didn't go she'd just be using Martin's death as an excuse. Looking at Traci she saw the pleading look in the other woman's eyes.

Cindy knew firsthand how hard it could be to deal with the trauma of finding a dead body. Anything she could do to make the next few days easier for Traci she should do. She slowly nodded. "Okay. If we're all agreed, then let's get this show on the road."

Fifteen minutes later she was regretting those words as she stood on the ground next to her horse. She was holding the reins in her left hand. She regarded her mount distrustfully. It was a tall horse, very beautiful and bright white. It eyed her, ears flicking back and forward and she felt like it was actually daring her to mount.

Kyle came over. “I picked the prettiest horse for you. I remembered how much you loved the Lone Ranger when we were kids. This horse is even named Silver after his horse. Beautiful, isn’t he?”

“He’s a bit tall,” Cindy admitted. “But he is very pretty,” she hastened to add.

“He can be a little on the spirited side, but I’m sure you’ll have no problems.”

Her mouth went dry. “I don’t think I can do this,” she said.

“Why, what’s wrong?”

“Kyle, I’ve never even been on a horse before. If I’m going to do this I need a nice, short, slow horse. I appreciate the thought, but I can’t ride this horse.”

He frowned. “I can switch horses with you today I guess until we get this sorted out. My horse is much shorter and from what I can tell pretty gentle.” His face lit up again. “This will work great, actually. Since I’m the host it makes more sense for me to be on the flashy horse anyway.”

“Yes, thank you,” she said, feeling relief flood through her.

He took the reins from her. “No problem. My horse, Petite, is right over there, the bay with the white stockings,” he said, pointing to a horse that was still standing, reins tied to the fence.

She turned and made her way to the horse. “Good, Petite,” she said when she got up close. She patted the animal’s neck gingerly and she didn’t move. Cindy took it as a good sign.

"You want me to show you how to mount?" Jeremiah asked, coming up beside her.

"That would be great."

"I can give you a boost or you can try to get up on your own," he said.

"How would I get up on my own?" she asked.

"Put your left foot in the stirrup, grab the reins and the pommel in your left hand, the back of the saddle with your right. Then bounce up and down on your right foot and then hoist yourself up."

Cindy realized very quickly that she was going to have to take up yoga or something when she got home. Just trying to get her foot up and into the stirrup proved challenging.

"Here, I'll just give you a boost," he said after a moment.

He bent down slightly and laced his fingers together. "Put your right foot in my hand and I'll give you a boost up. When you're on your stomach across the saddle, swing your right leg over and sit up."

"What if I just slide over the other side?" she asked dubiously.

"Don't worry, I won't let you."

Had it been anyone else telling her that she would have had her doubts, but she trusted Jeremiah. If he said he wouldn't let her fall off the other side then she wouldn't. She put her boot into his hands and he heaved her up in one quick, powerful movement.

A second later she found herself swinging her leg over and sitting up just as he had told her and she was on the horse. He helped her get her feet into both stirrups, adjusting the length for her. He showed her how to hold the reins in her right hand and when he was finished he stepped back.

She felt a momentary flare of panic as she realized it was just her and Petite.

"Now, to get her to back up, pull the reins straight back," he said.

She did and let out a little squeak of anxiety as the horse started walking backwards.

"Now relax them again."

She did and Petite stopped.

"Excellent. We'll make a rider of you yet," he told her with an encouraging smile.

She smiled hesitantly back then watched as he retrieved his own horse, a dark red one, and mounted in one smooth motion.

"That was impressive," she blurted out. "You must have ridden a lot."

He dropped his eyes to his horse. "Not much," he muttered, more to himself than her.

It seemed odd, almost like he didn't want to admit to having a lot of experience although the way he sat on the horse he looked as confident as the two cowboys who were already in their saddles.

"Looks like Mark finally made it onto his horse," he said. "I was beginning to think he was going to be riding backward today."

Cindy looked over at Mark and Traci and couldn't help but wonder if she looked as awkward on her horse as Mark looked on his. Traci, on the other hand, looked confident and happy. Cindy wished she knew what that felt like.

"Alright, everyone up on their horses," Kyle called, walking Silver down the line. "When we get about five miles out we'll be turning on our helmet cameras. That's when we'll be picking up the cattle. Alright, move 'em on out!"

The horses began to move forward, falling into a loose line and Cindy's stomach lurched as Petite took her place. *This is really happening*, she told herself. A moment later she could swear she heard someone singing Happy Trails and she found herself grinning.

Kyle swung up onto Silver and she had to admit that he looked good on top of the beautiful horse. She was surprised that he hadn't chosen him straight off. He had wanted her to have the pretty horse because she had liked The Lone Ranger. She was surprised that he remembered let alone cared. She stared at his back thoughtfully as he moved toward the front of the little cavalcade. Maybe the next few days would be a good thing, a chance to actually get to know her brother.

After what had happened to their sister when they were kids they had quickly grown apart as Cindy closed herself off and Kyle became more and more of a daredevil. She had always been so angry with him for taking stupid risks with his life. Then, eventually, she had forced herself to stop caring. Well, at least as much as she had. Then when her brother became famous and he was all her mother could talk about Cindy had let the anger over that color her feelings even more.

Maybe she'd been unfair to Kyle. He clearly cared about her. Sure, this whole stunt for his show would probably get him huge ratings but if it was just about that, he wouldn't have tried to give her Silver.

"What are you thinking?" Jeremiah asked.

She turned her head to see him riding beside her, easy in the saddle.

"That maybe my brother isn't the devil."

He smiled. "Wait, it's early yet."

She laughed at that. Jeremiah always seemed to know what to say to make things better. Her horse, Petite, seemed to be trying her best, too. She had a smooth walk and she seemed quite calm. She just followed along behind the horse in front of her without any steering from Cindy. She actually lifted her left hand off the pommel long enough to give the horse a swift pat on the neck.

"I know, he's got plenty of time to be the jerk I always think he is."

"Then again, maybe the two of you will get to bond some," Jeremiah said.

"I'm hoping," Cindy admitted. "I think his fans know him better than I do."

"Including Traci?" Jeremiah asked.

"Especially Traci," Cindy said with a grin as she noticed that the other woman was following right behind him, her horse's nose practically touching Silver's tail. "Should she be following that close?" she asked after a moment. She thought she remembered somebody saying something about trying to keep a horse-length between.

"No, but if it irritates his horse hers will get a swift kick for it," Jeremiah said.

"Ouch."

He shrugged.

After what seemed like just a couple of minutes Kyle halted and the rest of them came to a stop as well.

"The herd's just over that hill," he said, pointing to a small rise in front of them. "We're going to pick up the pace a bit. Now is the time to turn on your helmet cameras."

Cindy dutifully obliged, watching as everyone else did the same.

"Smile, you're on Candid Camera," she heard Mark say from behind her.

She shook her head, refusing to turn and look at him. She realized with a start that she suddenly had a bit of stage fright. Everything she said and did from this point forward would probably be recorded and could potentially be seen by millions of people. She felt her cheeks getting warm. She just hoped she didn't embarrass herself. She'd have to watch what she said and did. She could just imagine if she slipped up even a little how a couple of the people at the church would look at her.

Fortunately unless she did something totally out of character she figured that no one she actually worked with would care. Still, there were a couple of judgmental people she could think of who wouldn't hesitate to point out to her if she had done anything unchristian or unladylike. She wrinkled her nose at the thought then hastily tried to relax her facial features. People would wonder why she was making that face.

Stop being paranoid! she told herself.

"What's wrong?" Jeremiah asked.

Great. Now she'd have to admit it out loud.

"Just a little stressed out about being on camera," she said, forcing herself to try and smile at him. After all, his camera would be recording her since he was looking in her direction.

"Don't worry, I'm sure it will be fine," he said.

She wanted to ask him how he knew, but then people would wonder why she was paranoid about being on camera and would think she was hiding something.

How does Kyle live like this? she wondered.

Kyle kicked his horse forward into a trot and the other horses followed suit. Cindy hung on to the pommel, her stomach lurching as her horse jumped forward. The trot was a lot bumpier and she felt like her bones were being jostled together. Fortunately, it gave her something other than the cameras to fixate on.

They trotted swiftly up the hill and in a moment crested it. Cindy looked down into a valley and was awestruck as she saw hundreds of cattle dotting the grassy floor.

I'm really doing this, I'm really on a cattle drive.

She took in the scene below her and couldn't help but marvel. People had been doing this for hundreds of years. It was part of a long tradition, part of her heritage as an American. Now it was her turn to take part and experience what her ancestors might have. It took her breath away.

Somehow it hadn't been truly real to her until that moment. Despite all her fears and misgivings she felt a little thrill of excitement. She was going on a real adventure. She saw Traci trotting down the hill in front of her and heard Mark mutter something behind her. In that moment she decided she was going to live this adventure to its fullest. There were trained cowboys and a police officer, Escape! Channel employees, and Jeremiah there. What could possibly go wrong?

She began to trot down the hill. It took her a moment to adjust to the incline and to not feel like she was going to fall forward onto her horse's neck. The other horses were beginning to fan out, no longer following each other in single file and she saw the cowboys galloping ahead of the rest of them, streaking toward the herd, making high pitched whistling sounds as they did.

She turned Petite to follow Kyle who had headed his horse toward the left, realizing she had no clue where she was supposed to be or what exactly she was supposed to do. She glanced around and saw Jeremiah and his horse just behind her. Traci and Mark had brought their horses to a standstill and looked like they were talking to each other. She wondered if the sight of all the cattle in the valley had impressed them as much as it had her.

She turned her attention back to Kyle. He, too, had halted his horse and was half turning as though getting ready to address his followers.

She had almost reached him when her horse suddenly jumped to the side and made a screaming sound. A moment later Petite was rearing and Cindy's heart stopped as she tried to hold on for dear life. She thought for a moment the horse would fall over backward, crushing her underneath.

Petite plunged back to the ground and Cindy felt like she was falling sideways. She could see Kyle reaching for her horse's reins. He snatched at them but missed. Her horse bolted, running down the valley. She yanked back on the reins but it did nothing and then a moment later she realized she really was falling sideways.

She shrieked in terror as the saddle slid sideways and she went hurtling toward the ground.

4

Horrified, Jeremiah realized he couldn't stop Cindy from falling. All he could do was try his best to control it. Her saddle had slipped onto her horse's side and even as he was watching it came loose completely.

He stretched forward, pushing his own body out of his saddle as he did so. Thankfully his horse didn't shy, but continued to run the course Jeremiah had set for him. He snatched at the back of Cindy's shirt, snagging the collar with two fingers. He yanked as hard as he could, pulling her away from her horse's pounding hooves before he lost his hold and she fell onto the ground.

She fell hard, but at least it was on her side and not her head and it was away from her runaway mount who was already being run down by one of the cowboys.

Jeremiah reseated himself as he pulled his horse to a halt. As the animal stopped he jumped from the saddle and raced to Cindy's side, praying she was alright.

His heart stopped for a moment when she didn't move.

"Are you okay?" he asked as he dropped next to her. The saddle was still half between her knees. The foot that was on top was out of the stirrup and he carefully began to move the saddle. She groaned and her eyes flickered.

"Help here!" Jeremiah bellowed at the top of his lungs.

One of the younger members of the crew came racing up a few seconds later, face ashen. Before he could say anything Jeremiah barked instructions. "Hold this saddle just like this while I check on her other foot and see if it's stuck in the stirrup."

The man nodded and grasped the heavy saddle, doing his best to hold it steady despite the fact that his hands were shaking. Jeremiah carefully lowered himself down on the ground and lifted the saddle just enough so that he could see that her foot was indeed still caught in the stirrup.

"This will hurt," he told her.

Out of the corner of his eye he saw her nod understanding.

"Lift it a little, slowly, carefully," he instructed the other man who did as he was told.

"There, stop."

Jeremiah was able to reach in and pull the stirrup off of Cindy's foot, trying to keep from moving her foot as much as possible. When it was clear he nodded and the guy pulled the saddle away as Jeremiah lowered her foot onto the ground.

Immediately she began to try and sit up which relieved him. Out of the corner of his eye he saw the girth strap of the saddle swinging free. Something didn't look quite right to him.

"Just a second," he muttered to Cindy, hating to leave her side, but needing to take a quick look at the saddle before someone else did.

Cindy managed to make it to a sitting position just as Kyle came jogging up. He looked her over once and she could tell that he seemed relieved.

"You know what you do when you fall off a horse? You get right back on," Kyle said.

Cindy was sure that she was going to murder him in his sleep. Still, she accepted his hand up. She tried to stand, but fell back down onto the ground, nearly pulling him down with her.

"What's wrong?" Jeremiah asked, suddenly back by her side.

"My ankle hurts," Cindy admitted. "It didn't want to take my weight."

Kyle frowned. "I'll get the medic," he said.

He strode off quickly.

Cindy hadn't known they had a medic with them, and she was intensely grateful to hear that a medical professional would be able to check out her ankle.

Jeremiah knelt down next to her and carefully felt her ankle. She winced, and bit her lip.

"It doesn't feel broken," he said. "You probably just have a sprain."

"I hope so," she told him.

A few seconds later Kyle returned with one of the cowboys who dropped down next to her. She raised an eyebrow.

"Cindy this is Zack Matthews. Matthews, this is my sister, Cindy. She seems to have hurt her ankle."

"That was a nasty tumble you took," Zack said.

"You saw that?"

"Everyone saw that. You rode that horse like a champ, though."

"What made Petite freak out like that?" Cindy asked, trying not to wince as Zack prodded her left ankle.

"Turns out it was a snake, right there in the grass. They're not that common around here, but not unheard of," Kyle said with a frown. "She freaked, bolted, and then apparently the leather saddle strap was rotting and it just snapped. It was kind of like the perfect storm of accidents, really."

"From where I'm sitting there was nothing 'perfect' about it," Cindy said with a sigh.

She turned her attention back to the cowboy. "So, you're a medic?" she asked. "I thought you were a cowboy."

"I was raised on a ranch in northern California just outside of Amnesty. Went to school, became a doctor. Served two tours in Afghanistan and decided that I'd rather be a cowboy. Does this hurt?"

"Yes," she said, wincing.

"On a scale of one to ten?"

"Six."

He nodded, seemingly satisfied with her answer. Meanwhile she noticed that Jeremiah was frowning and staring at Kyle.

"The saddle strap broke?"

"Yeah, that's what it looks like," Kyle said. "So, how is she, Doc?"

"She'll be fine. She just needs a chance to heal up. It's a sprain. All things considered it's not nearly as bad as I would have thought. I reckon she's got you to thank for that," he said, turning to look at Jeremiah.

"We both got lucky," Jeremiah said shortly.

"What now?" Cindy asked no one in particular.

"Now, we get that foot elevated," Zack said.

"Aren't you going to tell me to get right back up on the horse?" she asked, realizing she was making a dig at her brother.

"Not with a sprained ankle. You'll just make it worse. No, you and Petite had a scare, you both deserve to rest. You can ride on the chuck wagon with Cookie and we'll tie Petite up behind so she can just walk along nice and slow."

Cindy was relieved beyond words. She didn't relish the thought of trying to get back on the horse, particularly with the way she felt.

Zack continued. "We'll go over, get you all set up with a pillow, some ice, and some painkillers. The good stuff. How does that sound?"

"At the moment, like as close to heaven as I'm going to get today," she said.

A dark cloud seemed to pass momentarily over Jeremiah's face. She wondered if her choice of words had been poor. Maybe she'd been in even more danger than she had thought. It wasn't good to dwell on that, though.

Mark was worried. It could have easily been Traci that had gotten hurt. Granted, his wife had a lot more experience with horses than he or Cindy. In fact, she probably could have brought the horse under control more quickly after the snake spooked it. Maybe she would have been able to figure out sooner that there was something wrong with the saddle, too. Still, that was a lot of "ifs" and "maybes" when it came to his wife's safety. To all of their safety for that matter.

This whole trip was starting to feel cursed and it was setting him on edge. As he was directed to take up position at the left side of the herd of cattle he couldn't help but wonder just how ineffectual he would be at keeping them in line, and whether or not anyone might get hurt because of that.

Fortunately, Traci had been assigned to the same general area as he was so he could keep an eye on her.

More like she can keep an eye on me, he realized as he uncomfortably moved his horse into a trot. He hated the pressure that the helmet was putting on his head, but he was also grateful for the protection. He figured it was only a matter of time before he got bucked off or thrown or just managed to lose his balance and he landed on his head.

Traci turned and gave him a radiant smile and he forced himself to smile back at her. Maybe he was crazy. Maybe they had just gotten all the trauma and drama out of the way and things would be smooth going from here on and out.

He heard a lot of loud calls and yip sounds and the herd of cattle began to slowly move down the valley. Ahead of him he saw one cow break ranks and watched in admiration as Traci moved to intercept it and turn it back.

After about ten minutes Kyle rode up beside him, startling him. It was all Mark could do not to cuss him out, reminding himself of the cameras on all their helmets.

"Everything going okay over here?" Kyle asked.

Mark nodded, still mindful of the camera. "Just where are we taking this herd?" he asked.

"To its winter pasture, a few days drive from here. Nearest town out there is Righteousness. That's where we'll end up and the trucks will take us home."

"Weird name for a town," Mark commented.

Kyle shrugged. "Settled by a bunch of religious folk about a hundred and fifty years ago. Still, I reckon I've heard stranger names."

Mark forced himself not to sneer when Kyle said "folk" and again when he said "reckon". The way he was speaking, he was clearly trying to sound western, like he was an old time cowboy himself. The affectation bothered Mark a bit. He tried to tell himself he needed to be more charitable, though. Kyle was an actor, after all, even if he did call himself an adventure guide or a travel host instead. The truth was, all the guys on camera at the Escape! Channel were actors first and foremost, whether they liked to admit it or not. It was their job to be entertaining and put on a bit of a show.

That, of course, led him to wonder how much of Kyle's on camera daring exploits weren't half so daring as they appeared. He couldn't help but think about Jeremiah saving that whole group of kids at the camp after they were attacked by assassins. How would Kyle have fared in a real life-and-death situation like that?

Of course, just thinking about that inevitably raised yet again the specter of his dead partner who had died trying to reach Jeremiah. Paul was the one mystery he couldn't let go of. He just hoped it wasn't also the one mystery that he could never solve.

Riding on the chuck wagon was turning out to be not only far more comfortable than riding on the horse but also far more entertaining. Chef Brent Joelson was turning out to be a fascinating conversationalist. Plus, he was giving her the inside scoop on all the inside details of the channel that her brother worked for. Some of his stories were so outrageous she had a hard time believing they were actually true.

He had just finished telling her how Bunni Sinclair had broken her leg in Guam and she felt terrible laughing so hard at someone else's misfortune. She couldn't help it, though. The story was so improbable and his telling of it so dramatic that she laughed until tears were streaming down her cheeks.

"Yeah, she has the worst luck of anyone I've ever met," Brent said at last.

"She's crazy to keep working there," Cindy said when she could finally breathe again.

"We all are. You know the host of the haunted house show?"

"The guy who looks like Malcolm McDowell?"

"That's the one."

"Doesn't believe in ghosts at all."

"Seriously? I thought I heard somewhere that he'd been communing with them his whole life."

"That's the hype, but it turns out he's a total skeptic. He finds the investigations completely boring but when the cameras are on he dutifully screams like a little girl."

Cindy found herself doubled over with laughter. "That's hilarious!"

"I know. I never miss one of his shows. And I never let him forget that he screams like a six year old with pigtails."

"Why does he do it?"

"It's a long story. I happen to know, though, that he'd like to host a much different show."

"And what's that?"

"Host a food show. He's a total foodie. A real gourmet."

"Which is why he doesn't kill you for teasing him."

"Exactly."

"I've never seen a food show on the channel," she admitted.

"There are only two. Mine which, of course, is marvelous."

"Of course," Cindy said, not bothering to hide her grin.

"And the other one."

"That doesn't sound good," she said.

He rolled his eyes. "The host, Janine Jefferson, is a junk food junkie. It breaks Malcolm's heart to watch her every time. If he was ever going to throttle someone at the network, it would be her."

"I'm surprised he doesn't," Cindy said.

"Ah, but I have a theory about that. I think he has feelings for her."

"So, he's not conflicted, not at all," she said sarcastically.

"That's us, one big dysfunctional family. We're the misfits, rejects and psychopaths of the travel industry."

"So, which one are you?" she asked before she could stop herself.

"Misfit. Definitely misfit."

"I wonder what Kyle is?" she mused.

He chuckled. "My dear he is definitely one of the psychopaths. One of these days he's going to get himself killed."

She blanched. It was bad enough that she thought that, but to hear it said by one of his colleagues just freaked her out that much more.

Brent glanced at her. "I'm sorry. I didn't mean to upset you."

"No, it's okay," she said hastily, not wanting to spoil the fun they were having.

"He's got a good team of people working with him. They make sure he stays safe. Plus, a lot of the things look a lot more dangerous on television than they actually are."

She couldn't help but think about her own recent accident. How would that look on television? Would it look worse than it had been? Living through it had been bad enough, she wasn't sure she'd want to watch it when it did air on television.

"I still can't believe I let him talk me into this," she said out loud.

"He's got a gift for that," Brent admitted.

Lunch arrived and it consisted of sandwiches that people could eat in their saddles if they chose to. After distributing them along with more bottled water Brent settled back down on the seat next to Cindy.

"It's a concession," he admitted. "I didn't see most of this crew faring too well with some kind of beef jerky."

"I know that I, for one, am thrilled to have the roast beef," she said.

"Me, too. Dollars to donuts, though, that this never makes it onto television. People will think I starved everyone until dinner. Everything around here is ninety percent perception and ten percent reality." He actually sounded a little bitter as he said the last.

Cindy resisted the urge to pat him on the shoulder. "Well, at least I know the truth. And the truth is, this is an amazing sandwich."

When they finally stopped for the night Mark practically fell off his horse. He was sore in muscles he never knew he had and his backside wasn't about to forgive him anytime soon. He did his best not to think about the fact that he'd have to do it all over again the next day even as he tried to stay upright on legs that were suddenly incredibly wobbly.

"Takes a while to get used to for a city slicker like you," one of the cowboys noted with thinly veiled sarcasm.

Mark noticed that the cowboy was carrying a gun. That was good. Mark was, too, and this way if he shot the man he could claim some sort of self-defense.

He walked over to Traci as she dismounted from her horse and he was gratified to see that her legs looked a little wobbly, too.

"I've never been in the saddle that long at one stretch," she admitted with a laugh as she reached out and grabbed onto his shoulder.

She was laughing which meant she was having a good time. That made him feel a bit better. Then he saw Jeremiah walking toward them, no signs of wobbly legs at all. Mark hated him in that moment. He also couldn't help but wonder if the rabbi had spent more time on horseback than he'd led the rest of them to believe.

"You grow up on a ranch?" Mark asked him.

"No."

That was it, just the one word. He was actually surprised he'd gotten that much out of him. Jeremiah didn't talk about his past. Mark knew nothing about him from before he had become a rabbi in Pine Springs. It was only out of respect that he hadn't gone digging. Plus, he wasn't sure he'd like what he found.

Together the three of them walked over to the chuck wagon where everyone seemed to be congregating. The chef was already in the back, hard at work on dinner. At least, that's what Mark hoped was happening.

"You okay?" Jeremiah asked Cindy, the worry in his voice clear.

"Yes. Glad to have stopped bouncing around. It was starting to get wearing," she admitted.

Mark kept a snarky comment to himself. Given what had happened to her earlier he wouldn't want to trade places with her even if riding on the wagon sounded a whole lot better than riding on a horse.

Dinner was not nearly as festive an affair as it should have been. Given the things that had happened and the pure exhaustion he knew he personally was feeling Mark wasn't surprised. Kyle, though, kept going around making jokes trying to get people to lighten up. Even he finally gave up after a while, though, and suggested that maybe it was a good idea if everyone turned in early and got some sleep. It was the most sense he'd made all day.

They laid out their sleeping bags all close together. The real cowboys were going to take turns watching the herd that night, although Kyle made it clear that starting the following night everyone was going to get a chance to pull night duty.

Mark finally stretched out in his sleeping bag next to Traci who had already burrowed into her bag. She was the only one in the group smiling and he was grateful she was enjoying herself. On her other side was Cindy and Jeremiah's sleeping bag was next, although the rabbi was nowhere to be seen. As he heard Cindy and Traci whispering together Mark felt himself began to drift off to sleep.

He didn't know how long he had been out, but the camp was quiet when a strong hand on his shoulder shook him awake. It was Jeremiah, still fully dressed. He put a finger to his lips indicating silence and gestured for Mark to follow him.

Mark got up and followed quietly until they were well out of earshot of the rest. Finally Jeremiah stopped and turned to look at him.

"What is it?" he asked.

"I wanted a chance to talk when I knew there were no cameras around," Jeremiah said.

"Fair enough, but about what? What are we doing out here?" Mark asked.

"I managed to get a look at Cindy's saddle. The leather didn't look rotted to me."

"You think someone saddled the horse wrong or missed seeing frayed edges, some sort of negligence?" Mark asked.

Jeremiah shook his head. "I don't think so."

Mark paled. "Why, why would anyone do that to Cindy? I mean, sure, it's going to make great television, but I have a hard time believing Kyle would risk his sister getting hurt just to add some drama. He's a jerk, but not that much of a jerk."

Jeremiah shook his head. "Kyle was supposed to be riding the horse, not Cindy. They switched at the last minute."

Mark frowned. "What are you saying?"

Jeremiah took a deep breath, realizing that once the words were out there was no taking them back. "I think someone tried to kill Kyle."

5

Mark stared hard at Jeremiah. "You're sure?"

"Not one-hundred percent, but worried enough to talk to you about it."

"That's good enough for me," Mark said, licking his lips. "You think that what happened to that cameraman back at the cabin wasn't an accident?"

"You tell me," Jeremiah said quietly.

Mark's mind raced. "He was roughly the same height and size as Kyle, and if I remember correctly their bunks were next to each other."

"You think in the dark someone mistook him, slammed his head into that sink?" Jeremiah asked.

Mark swore under his breath. "I hope for all our sake's you're wrong." In his gut, though, he felt that Jeremiah was on to something. He glanced back over his shoulder. "Should we warn Kyle?"

"It would be the logical thing to do. Except..."

"Except what?" Mark asked when Jeremiah didn't finish his thought.

"I'm not sure it would make much of a difference. I don't think he'd cancel this cattle drive. If anything it might just make him act strange and alert whoever it is that we're on to them."

"Which means we'd never find the killer and there'd be no justice for the guy he already killed."

"And, if he's someone that has access to Kyle, he'll just try again in a few weeks when no one's watching out for him and he's let his guard down."

"We've gotten ourselves in the middle of a fine mess," Mark snorted.

"Don't we always?" Jeremiah said grimly.

Mark glanced over his shoulder again. "What about Traci and Cindy? We should warn them."

"We should."

There was a lack of conviction in Jeremiah's voice that matched his own feeling. "Then they'll be the jumpy ones instead of Kyle."

"That is a risk," Jeremiah said.

"Well, crap. What are we supposed to do?"

"Make sure one of us has eyes on Kyle the entire time?"

Mark nodded. The rabbi's suggestion made perfect sense. He wished suddenly and intensely that he was a praying man. "Do me a favor, Samaritan," he said, using the sarcastic nickname he had given Jeremiah ages ago.

"What?"

"Pray enough for both of us. Pray that we're wrong about this whole thing."

Cindy woke up and blinked up at the night sky. She couldn't have been asleep very long, but it felt like the temperature had dropped considerably in that time. She rolled over and noticed that Jeremiah's sleeping bag was empty. He was probably just getting a drink of water or something like that, but for some reason it made her uneasy. Maybe it was because of what had happened at the cabin the night before.

She propped herself up on one elbow and twisted her head so she could look around. Everywhere there was a sea of sleeping bags. Next to her Traci was sleeping with one hand flung over her eyes. On the other side of her, Mark's sleeping bag was empty, too.

Cindy sat up, coming fully awake. One missing guy could be a trip to the bathroom. Two missing guys seemed like danger to her. She looked around, checking all the other sleeping bags she could see.

The moon was full and shining down brightly enough that she could count heads. Everyone else seemed to be accounted for except for the cowboy she knew was supposed to be taking the first shift watching the herd. Wherever Jeremiah and Mark had gone, though, they were out of sight.

She started to throw back her sleeping bag and the blanket she had over it and then hesitated. Where would she begin to look for them?

"Where do you think they've gone?" Traci whispered so suddenly that Cindy jumped and nearly screamed.

"Sorry," Traci said.

"It's okay," Cindy whispered back. "I don't know where they went."

"They've been gone about ten minutes. I was starting to wonder what's up."

"Yeah, guys don't go to the bathroom in groups," Cindy muttered.

"But girls do."

As if reading each other's minds they both got up at the same time. Cindy winced, reaching for the walking stick Jeremiah had found for her after dinner. Her ankle was still sore even though the pain medication Zack had given her was pretty effective.

She hobbled slowly alongside Traci and they didn't speak a word until they were out of earshot of the sleeping figures.

"Anyone who's watching should think we're just heading for the bathroom," Traci said. "Actually, now that I'm up, that doesn't seem like such a bad idea. I don't want to have to go at like four in the morning."

"Are you sure my brother won't have us up at four in the morning anyway?" Cindy asked.

"He's crazy. I'm hoping he's not *that* crazy," Traci said.

"So, where do you think the guys went?" Cindy asked, bringing them back to the topic at hand.

"Do you think they're investigating the murder of the cameraman?" Traci asked, eyes widening.

"What? No, he wasn't murdered," Cindy said.

"Are you so sure?"

"Yes, why? Do you think he was murdered?"

Traci nodded. "The more I think about it, the more I'm convinced he must have been."

That got Cindy's attention. "Really, why?"

"Because even if something looks like an accident, if someone dies and you and Jeremiah are around, it wasn't."

Cindy fought the urge to laugh at the sheer preposterousness of the other woman's reasoning. Then she realized Traci wasn't smiling. She looked dead serious.

"There must be more to it than that," Cindy said cautiously.

"No, just that, and a feeling I guess."

"Feelings aren't something to be ignored," Cindy said. She'd learned that, if nothing else, through all her misadventures. "Okay, so who do you think killed him and why?"

"That's what I want to figure out. You're so good at this I was sure you'd have a theory already."

Cindy shook her head. "To be honest, I was happy with the 'just an accident' theory. I'd like to live my life without getting sucked into any more of these situations."

"Somehow I think the universe has other plans."

"You mean God keeps putting me in these situations for a reason?" Cindy mused.

Traci shrugged. "I don't know anything about God, but I do know that you've been involved in too many of these things for it to be coincidence. I think God or fate or whatever wants you to get involved, lend a hand. I mean, who knows how many more people would have died over the last couple of years if you hadn't been around helping to solve these things."

"Don't let your husband hear you say that."

"Mark's happy for the help, but he would never admit it." She sighed. "I just wish you could help him figure out the whole mystery of who Paul really was."

"I've heard a little about that," Cindy admitted.

"It's driving him crazy, to be honest. He's become so obsessed with it it's hard for him to focus on anything else."

Cindy reached out and gave Traci a quick hug. "I'm sorry," she whispered.

"Thanks," Traci said, pulling back after a moment. "But now, back to the task at hand, who do you think killed that guy?"

"I don't know who might be trying to kill Kyle," Jeremiah said to Mark.

The detective sighed. “Who wouldn’t want to kill him might be a better question. I know I’ve harbored murderous thoughts a couple times in the past day and I don’t even know the guy.”

Jeremiah bit back a chuckle.

“I have a feeling I’m not the only one,” Mark commented.

Jeremiah shook his head, but didn’t say anything.

“Shouldn’t you be on your best behavior, you know, given that he’s the first family member of Cindy’s that you’ve met?”

“What do you mean?” Jeremiah asked.

“Please, don’t give me that. It’s not quite meeting the parents, but it’s certainly a step in that direction.”

Jeremiah rolled his eyes. “There’s nothing going on between Cindy and me.”

“Whether there is or not isn’t the point. There should be and you know it and I know it. You can’t tell me you’re not the least little bit trepidatious about spending time with one of her relatives.

“She’s not very fond of her brother.”

“And you’re dodging the question. Whether she likes him or not doesn’t mean anything. You know he’s got to be sizing you up and that he’ll be reporting back to mom and dad about the guy she’s been spending all her time with.”

Jeremiah could feel his temper slipping. It didn’t help that Mark was right about that last part. He had worried about what Kyle might say to Cindy’s parents and whether or not they might object to her spending so much time with him. What made it worse was that he wasn’t sure whether or not Cindy would care what they thought. He wasn’t about to let Mark know he had struck a nerve, though.

"How about we get back to figuring out who's trying to kill Kyle and worry about Cindy's parents later," he suggested.

"You do care, I knew it," Mark said, a smug sound to his voice.

"What I care about is all of us making it through the next few days alive," Jeremiah said.

"Okay, fine," Mark said, sounding clearly disappointed. Apparently the detective would rather discuss Jeremiah's love life than stop a killer. Maybe he was taking the whole vacation concept a little too far.

"So, despite how we all feel about Kyle, I think it's safe to eliminate the four of us as potential suspects," Jeremiah said.

Mark snorted. "Yeah, only worry from Traci is that she might hug him to death."

Jeremiah bit back a sarcastic comment which would only lead Mark back onto the topic of relationships.

"The three cowboys weren't bunking with us at the cabin when the cameraman was killed," Jeremiah said instead.

"Yeah, what are their names again?" Mark asked.

"Zack is the doctor, Tex is the older one and Curly is the younger one," Jeremiah said.

"Curly? Are you kidding me?"

"No, why?"

"Curly? Come on, the guy must have seen City Slickers one too many times as a kid and decided that Jack Palance was the god of all things cowboy."

Jeremiah hadn't seen the film in question. He had just assumed the nickname had to do with the young man's extremely curly hair. He felt like he had done a pretty good job assimilating into American culture but every so often there were pop culture references he just did not get. It reminded him that he was an outsider, not really part of this world.

And unable to go back to his.

He shook his head. "So, unless one of them knew Kyle prior to this, I'm betting we can rule them out."

"Someone could have hired one of them to go after him."

"True, but I kind of doubt it."

"Yes, because you've never met a hired killer before," Mark said, sarcasm dripping from his voice.

Jeremiah stiffened slightly until he realized Mark was referencing the Green Pastures incident from Saint Patrick's Day.

"One of them could have snuck into the cabin and they all had access to the saddle and could have cut the girth strap. Okay, so let's not rule them out completely," Jeremiah said.

"Done. So, moving on to the people Kyle brought with him, other than us, of course."

"Hank and Norman arrived the next morning to replace Martin and the guy Aaron who left afterward."

"I'd say we should be wondering if Aaron killed Martin but he was long gone by the time those horses were saddled up," Mark said. "And, you're right, Hank and Norman might have been able to do something to the saddle, but they weren't even here when Martin got killed."

"Still, they managed to get both of them here really quickly. I wonder where they were coming in from," Jeremiah mused more to himself than Mark.

Mark shrugged. "What about Liz, the hair and make-up lady. I've got to say, I don't know what they brought her along on this trip for."

"Close-ups and things like that in the camp?" Jeremiah guessed.

"Could be. Okay, moving on. We have our cook, Brent. Think he resents being a gourmet chef and being stuck on a chuck wagon as a stunt?"

"He could, but would he really resort to murder to get this whole thing shut down? I mean, why not just sabotage?"

"You're right. Yeah, whoever it is probably has a grudge against Kyle and not the production. That's the way it's seeming, after all. Although, we could be wrong."

"So, that leaves us with three more guys, Jeremiah said. "Roddy is Kyle's assistant."

"Imagine having that job. I'm sure he has plenty of reasons to want to kill the guy."

"And the last two are Wayne and Junior."

"Father and son, aren't they?" Mark asked.

"I think so."

"And what exactly is it they do?"

"I get the impression a little of everything, hauling equipment, running errands and messages. I think they were even the ones that did the majority of the work setting up the camp."

"So, do we know if any of these guys has worked with Kyle before, maybe on one of his other shows?" Mark asked.

"I'm not sure," Jeremiah said. "I would think so, but I don't know for sure. We'd have to ask him."

"We have to find a good way to do it without arousing his suspicions just yet."

"Have Traci ask. He knows she's a fan and it would be natural for her to want to know more about the behind the scenes things."

Jeremiah heard Mark growl low in his throat at that suggestion.

"You're right," Mark finally admitted with a sigh. "Let's head back to camp. I'll talk to her in the morning. I've got to be careful about that, too, though. She was upset enough about finding Martin's body. I don't want to do anything to ruin this trip for her."

"Her favorite celebrity getting killed could do that," Jeremiah pointed out.

"I know," Mark groused. "Time is of the essence. That's why we need to get back and get some sleep."

"This is the first episode for a new show, right?" Cindy asked.

"Yes, episode one of Wild Escape! How did you not know that?" Traci asked.

Cindy winced. "I'm not the fan you are."

"His shows are fantastic. You really should watch them," Traci said.

"You sound like my mom."

"Sorry. Okay, no more nagging."

"Thanks. So, Kyle seemed to know Martin pretty well. I'm guessing he'd worked with him on one of his previous shows. I guess the question is, does any of the other crew also have past experience with Martin?"

"Maybe one of them killed him because of it?" Traci asked.

"That's what I'm wondering."

"I can find out, ask Kyle about the behind the scenes of how his shows worked, find out who's new to his crew and who might have had a grudge against Martin."

"That would be great," Cindy said. "You're a fan, so he'll totally eat up the attention and tell you everything we need to know."

"It might have been that other guy who left already," Traci mused.

"That would be better for us," Cindy said.

"How so?" Traci asked.

"Because if it wasn't that guy, then we're stuck out here in the middle of nowhere with a killer."

There was a moment of silence as they both let that sink in. Suddenly the night seemed a little darker, a little more ominous to Cindy. She could feel herself beginning to panic a little and she forced herself to take long, calming breaths. She grabbed a section of her fleecy pajama bottoms between her thumb and forefinger and began to rub it, forcing herself to focus on the tactile sensation and not on the anxiety that was flooding her system.

"I'm sorry, I didn't mean to stress you out," Traci said quietly after a moment.

"It's not your fault," Cindy said. "It's just something I have to deal with."

The truth was she would be incredibly happy when she could stop dealing with it. It wasn't that simple, though. The PTSD she was suffering from had a mind of its own and seemed to strike when and where it liked. She had learned though that trying to keep her mind in the present moment helped tremendously.

Slowly she felt herself beginning to calm down. “So, the word of the day is caution,” she said at last. “We could be totally wrong about all of this.”

“We could also be totally right,” Traci said quietly. “Mark’s already so stressed out I don’t think I want to tell him our suspicions just yet.”

“Okay,” Cindy agreed. “We can go to him when, if, we get more.”

“Until then we just need to stay alert and keep our eyes open.”

“Agreed.”

“Okay, I’ll stick close to my guy and you stick close to yours,” Traci said.

“I-I don’t have a guy,” Cindy stammered.

Traci rolled her eyes. “Oh, please. I can’t believe the two of you haven’t figured it out yet.”

“Figured what out?” Cindy asked, heart beginning to race.

“That you and Jeremiah are perfect for each other.”

“What? No, we’re just friends,” Cindy managed to say, grateful that the night kept Traci from seeing that she was blushing. Her mind had begun to race and she felt her pulse skittering out of control at the very thought.

“You might be friends, but you’re meant to be a whole lot more. I guarantee it,” Traci said with a certainty that made Cindy’s heart pound even harder.

“But, we’re all wrong for each other,” she protested. “I’m not looking for a guy like him.”

Traci snorted derisively. “Yeah, what kind of guy are you looking for?”

The question caught her off guard and Cindy realized she had no good way to answer it. She licked her lips. "He's Jewish and I'm a Christian," she finally blurted out.

"Yeah, and Mark wasn't anything I was looking for in the slightest and yet there you go."

Cindy didn't know how to answer that without venturing more into the religious differences territory. Instead she said, "Jeremiah's not interested in me in that way."

"Hmm, funny that you say he's not interested instead of saying you aren't," Traci said.

Cindy blinked in surprise. Traci was right. Her first response should have been that she wasn't interested. It hadn't been. What did that mean?

"And besides, what makes you think he isn't interested?" Traci pushed.

Cindy pressed her hands to her burning cheeks. "I don't want to talk about this," she whispered. It was true. She couldn't, wouldn't discuss this right now with Traci. Clearly she had some feelings she had to sort out for herself before she'd be willing to discuss them with anyone. Just because she'd vowed to try and make this a good trip for Traci it didn't mean she had to bare her soul to her. Not like this.

"We should get back then," Traci said, sounding a bit disappointed.

Cindy couldn't help that. Although she found herself suddenly wishing that her cell phone worked out here so she could call her roommate Geanie. In the next breath she realized that would be just as big a mistake. Geanie was engaged and to her love was in the air. She couldn't be practical about these sorts of things at the moment if her life depended on it.

"Yeah, hopefully they haven't sent out a search party for us," Cindy muttered.

"If they're not in their sleeping bags when we get back, we're sending a search party out for them," Traci said firmly.

They had taken less than half a dozen steps when a shadow suddenly loomed over them. Cindy took a hasty step backward.

"You ladies aren't supposed to be here," a deep voice growled.

6

They had reached the sleeping area when Mark stopped short.

"What is it?" Jeremiah whispered.

"Girls are gone," Mark said, hating the tension in his own voice. He forced himself to take a deep breath. "Maybe they went looking for us. Or, maybe they just had to relieve themselves."

"Is everyone here except the cowboy on guard duty?" Jeremiah asked.

Mark squinted into the darkness. "Looks like it, so, unless there's someone else stalking us from outside everything should be okay."

He heard himself talking and couldn't help but wonder when he'd gotten so paranoid. Didn't he even know how to relax anymore?

"Actually, Hank is missing. His sleeping bag is empty," Jeremiah whispered.

Mark swore under his breath and glanced at the rabbi who was pointing at a spot at the edge of the camp.

"You can see that far in this light, let alone remember who was over there?"

Jeremiah didn't answer. It just reinforced Mark's growing belief that the other man saw and heard a lot more than he ever let on. He had the senses of a fox and twice the craftiness.

Hank was one of the new guys, just arrived that morning. Still, that didn't make Mark feel any better knowing that he was out there somewhere and so were Traci and Cindy.

"I don't like this," he muttered.

He turned around and swore again. Jeremiah was gone.

Cindy heard Traci gasp even as she craned her neck to try and make out the face of the man confronting them. She recognized the chiseled features of the new assistant cameraman, Hank.

"What do you mean?" she managed to ask without stammering. In her mind she quickly ran through their options. The guy was massive, Traci and she wouldn't stand much of a chance trying to fight him. That left running and screaming for help that would hopefully arrive in time. Of course, with her ankle the way it is, even that wasn't a good option.

"We won't tell anyone," she heard Traci practically whisper. "We're very sorry. We have very vivid imaginations, you know?"

Hank eyed them and then crossed his thick, corded arms over his chest. "Then you can imagine how much trouble you'd be in if you got lost out here in the middle of the night."

This was it. Cindy tensed, getting ready to leap away and prayed that Traci would follow. She wrapped her hand tight around her walking stick, praying she'd be able to use it to help her move fast enough.

"You're headed straight out for the herd, away from camp," he said. "You get lost, start fumbling around, risk spooking those cattle and you'll be in serious trouble."

Cindy stared at him, feeling like an idiot. “We’re going the wrong way for camp?”

“If that’s where you’re heading.”

“But, I thought it was over that way,” she said pointing.

“Out here in the wilderness, in the dark, without landmarks you know or understand, it’s easy to get turned around,” he said. “You ladies want to go back that way,” he said, pointing behind them.

“Thank you,” Traci gasped, clearly feeling the same relief Cindy was.

A terrible suspicion suddenly dawned on her. What if he was lying to them, trying to get them lost?

Either way, their best bet was to go in the direction he was telling them. If he was being truthful he would have saved them. If he was lying they could hopefully figure it out quickly and circle back without risking confronting him now.

“We appreciate the help,” Cindy asked, forcing herself to smile, biting her tongue to keep from asking him what exactly he was doing away from camp himself. She wasn’t sure questioning him at the moment was smart, especially if he in turn began to question them.

She grabbed Traci’s hand, turned and began to walk in the direction he had indicated. Traci’s grip was like steel and she could practically feel the other woman’s fear radiating off of her.

After taking a dozen steps she risked looking back over her shoulder. She couldn’t see Hank anymore and she tried not to let her imagine get the best of her in wondering where he’d gone.

After a dozen more steps Traci whispered, “Do you think we’re really going in the right direction?”

Before she could answer, Cindy saw a shape walking toward them in the darkness. Whoever it was was tall, but not as tall as Hank. Before she could hail them, she heard a familiar voice call out.

"Everything okay?"

She nearly dropped Traci's hand and ran forward to hug Jeremiah. She managed to restrain herself, though, and she took one last look behind them. There was still no sign of Hank.

"Um, yeah, we're fine. Hank helped send us back in the right direction," she said.

"Allow me to escort you the rest of the way," Jeremiah said, his voice tense even though his words were not.

Less than a minute later they were back in camp and standing next to Mark. Mark glared briefly at Jeremiah although Cindy had no idea why.

"Found them," Jeremiah said shortly.

"We figured you went to use the little girl tree," Mark said.

"Nice, honey," Traci said sarcastically.

"What? That's as delicately as I could put it," he said.

He was trying to look innocent, but Cindy suspected that he was lying. There was a muscle in his jaw that was twitching.

He thought something bad happened to us, she realized.

She couldn't blame him. Between her and Traci they had been kidnapped three times in the last year. That was more than enough to make anyone twitchy.

"So, how about we all do what we're supposed to be doing and get some sleep?" he said.

"Sounds good to me," Cindy replied, wishing briefly that she and Traci had made it to the little girl's tree as Mark put it.

She got back in her sleeping bag which was now cold and pulled the top of the bag and the blanket up under her chin. Traci was seconds behind her followed by Mark.

Jeremiah continued to stand for a couple minutes more, looking around. Cindy wondered if he was looking for Hank, but she held her tongue and didn't ask. The last thing she wanted was for him to feel the need to go looking for the big man. He might not be the killer that she and Traci were looking for, but they couldn't rule anyone out at this point. The fact that he had been skulking around in the dark didn't make him any more innocent in her eyes.

Then again, from his point of view, maybe she and Traci were the ones skulking. She sighed, wishing that just for once things could be simple and people's motives completely transparent.

She was nearly asleep when Jeremiah finally decided to turn in. As he settled into his sleeping bag next to hers Cindy felt her heart begin to pound again. He had been close to her in the cabin, but this seemed even closer, more intimate. Her sleepiness vanished and she felt wide awake.

"Night, Cindy," he whispered.

"Goodnight, Jeremiah," she barely managed to get out around the sudden tightness in her chest.

She listened as a few minutes later his breathing slowed and deepened as did Traci's on her other side. Finally, what seemed like a lifetime later, she was able to fall asleep herself.

Jeremiah was up early. He wanted to take another look around the camp in the early morning light before the others were awake. Zack was the only other one awake and he was out tending to the herd. Jeremiah could hear snatches of cowboy songs floating on the air and couldn't help but wonder if the doctor turned cowboy hadn't missed his true calling as a singer.

Hank was asleep. The man had returned to camp shortly before Jeremiah had turned in, moving so silently even Jeremiah hadn't been able to hear him. He had seen him, though, and he knew the other man had seen him as well. The two of them were going to have to have a little chat about what he had been doing up so late and for so long at some point.

With no one around to question him he was able to inspect the remaining saddles, although he intended to inspect Kyle's again before the ride began for the day, just to be certain it hadn't been tampered with.

Everything seemed to be in order and after a while the other two cowboys stirred and got up. They both nodded to him as they went about their preparations.

Jeremiah went over and quietly began to roll up his sleeping bag, not wanting to disturb Cindy. He knew she couldn't have gotten very much sleep. She had still been wide awake when he'd finally let himself go to sleep. He'd wanted to remain awake until she had fallen asleep, but had ultimately decided that getting the hours he'd need to be alert today were more important. Besides, she was sleeping so near him that if she had tried to get up again he would have known it instantly.

She finally awoke, blinking slowly. Then she smiled up at him and he felt warm to the center of his being.

"Morning, sleepy," he said.

"What time is it?" she asked.

"A bit after six."

She yawned. "That's early."

"Yup. You're not the last one up, though."

"I bet Kyle is awake."

"Yes, and already hard at work," Jeremiah noted.

Cindy rolled her eyes.

It only took Cindy a few minutes to get dressed and be ready for the day to begin. She had just heard that breakfast wouldn't be ready for about another twenty minutes when she saw Kyle approaching her.

"Hey, sis. Care to take a walk with me, or a hobble with me at least?" he asked.

She nodded. She had been getting along okay that morning without the makeshift walking stick as long as she moved slow.

She couldn't help but wonder what it was Kyle wanted, though, as they began walking slowly away from the camp.

"How are you feeling this morning?"

"Better, I can put weight on my ankle, but it's sore still."

"Best to rest it up at least another day," he said, surprising her slightly.

"Thanks."

"I'm sorry that you got hurt. It should have been me on that horse," he said, sounding guilty.

She reached out a hand to grab his arm. "It's okay, you couldn't have known."

He nodded. “It’s just strange. First Martin, then that. Last night I was beginning to think this trip was cursed.”

“And now?”

“The dawn brings with it optimism the night could never dream of,” he said.

“That’s beautiful.”

“Thanks. I stole it from a girl I dated in college.”

She nodded, not sure what to say. The silence stretched on as clearly he didn’t know what else to say either.

“So, Mom tells me you have a new girlfriend,” Cindy said, looking for something to fill the silence. “Last year apparently you took her over there for Thanksgiving if I remember correctly.”

“You know, you could show up to Thanksgiving every once in a while,” Kyle said.

“Is that your way of avoiding the topic?”

“I don’t know, maybe. I just don’t want you to get all weirded out.”

“I’m not going to get weirded out hearing about your girlfriend,” Cindy said.

“Okay. She’s a year younger than I am and she’s an interior designer although that doesn’t even begin to cover it. She’s amazing and she can do anything from renovate a house to make a gourmet dinner for twenty. I swear, she’s like the next Martha Stewart.”

“Hopefully without the prison record,” she couldn’t help but snark.

He looked at her and she felt bad. That hadn’t been a nice thing to say, especially when he was trying to be open with her.

“I’m sorry, go on,” she said.

"We met a little over a year ago while I was on location in Prague. She was there on vacation and it was just...magic."

"That sounds really nice. Does she live near you?"

"That's the freaky part. Only twenty minutes away and yet we had to go all the way to Prague to meet."

"Sometimes that's how it is with people who lead such busy lives," Cindy said. "Not everyone is lucky enough to just bump into their next door neighbor and fall in love."

"You seem to have been."

"Excuse me?" she asked.

"Hello, the rabbi? Earth to Cindy. Can you read me?"

"I can read you just fine," she said, feeling her blood pressure rise. "But you're not making any sense. I'm not in love with Jeremiah."

Kyle looked at her confused. "It's not the cop then, is it, because he's married and that's not cool."

"I'm not in love with Mark!" she burst out horrified, and then felt her cheeks burn as she realized how loudly she had said that. Half the camp had probably heard.

He frowned. "Well, it must be Jeremiah, because it's got to be someone. Mom always says when a woman is in love you can tell because she has a glow about her and you're glowing, that's for sure. I've never seen you like this before."

"Maybe it's just because you haven't seen me in years. I've changed a lot, you know."

He didn't say anything and she forced herself to take a deep breath. He hadn't done anything wrong, after all. Maybe she did glow. She was certainly happier than she had been the last time they'd seen each other. A lot had changed in her life since then. Her eyes drifted toward the camp and she realized she was looking for Jeremiah.

She looked hastily back at her brother, not wanting him to notice what she was doing. She forced herself to unclench her fists and did her best to calm herself down. "So, are you in love?" she asked.

"I think so," he said, his voice getting a little hoarse. "It's all kind of weird and new to me, but I think it's possible that she could be the one."

"Fangirls the world over will be crushed to hear that," she said, forcing a smile.

He shrugged.

"So, what is her name?"

He fidgeted for a moment, dropping his eyes, then sighed. "Her name is Lisa."

Cindy felt as though something exploded inside her. "Are you kidding me?" she hissed.

"Now, hold on, I know what you're going to say-"

"You're dating someone with the same name as our dead sister. That's wrong! Wrong and creepy! You just-you just can't replace her."

"I'm not trying to replace her. Crap, this is exactly what I was talking about, Cind, about not wanting you to go all mental and freak out."

"I'm not the mental one, that would be you."

"Really, because what you're doing now, that's insane. You're not being rational. It's just a name. They don't even look alike, not really."

"Not really? What does that mean? What, do they have the same hair color, eye color?"

"No, nothing like that," he said, raising his hands as though to fend off her questions.

"I can't believe you! And you weren't going to tell me. What, were you saving that surprise for the wedding invitation?"

"Listen to me, Cindy. Lisa, our sister, she's dead, and there's nothing we can do to bring her back."

"You don't think I don't know that?" She was yelling. She could hear herself, but somehow she couldn't force herself to lower her voice as she just kept going. "I live with that every single day."

"And you don't honor her by shutting yourself up away from the world and not living your own life!" Kyle was shouting now, too.

"Oh, and you honor her by stupidly risking your life on all these crazy stunts?"

"More than you!"

Cindy swung her fist and hit Kyle as hard as she could in the face.

He staggered backward, a look of shock on his face.

Then she felt hands grabbing her shoulders, dragging her away from him. She was shaking with rage and something else that she realized must be shock. A moment later she was sitting cross-legged on the ground, head in her hands.

"Seems to me we've been down this road before," Mark said. "Only last time all you did was slap Jeremiah. Seems you're graduating. That was a nice punch, by the way, I'm just sorry I wasn't the one who threw it."

She looked up at him after a minute. "I hit him," she said.

"I know. You're still working your way through the PTSD. You're going to lose it every once in a while, the trick is just learning to control the direction in which you lash out."

"This had nothing to do with PTSD and everything to do with Kyle," she said.

"I'm sure he deserved it."

"He's dating a woman with the same first name as our dead sister."

Mark blinked at her. "Okay. I can see where that might be a bit traumatic to someday have to reference her as your sister or sister-in-law, or whatever."

He didn't get it, she could tell. She could also tell he wasn't about to say so, probably afraid that she would hit him as well.

She was tired. At the moment it felt like that was all she had ever been her entire life was tired. The thought of spending another day being bounced around on the wagon sounded like more than she could take. "I don't think I'm cut out to be a cowboy," she admitted.

"Well, you hit like one," Jeremiah said as he walked up, looking inordinately pleased.

"What is it?" she asked.

"Kyle's going to be doing the rest of his show with a magnificent black eye."

She knew she should feel guilty. Knew it, wanted to, but couldn't. Instead she felt a strong sense of satisfaction. This day had been coming for a lot of years. She had finally told her brother off and hit him in the eye with a fist instead of a dart like she had for years with her dartboard back home.

It didn't make her feel any better about him dating a woman named Lisa, but it did make her feel a bit better about everything else. Even a long day on the wagon didn't seem so bad now that she knew Kyle would have a black eye while on television. Of course, there was a chance that Liz could work wonders with her make-up kit, but she hoped not.

In fact, she happened to know that Liz's kit was riding in the back of the chuck wagon with some of the other equipment that was too large to carry on horseback. Maybe if she accidentally bumped it and it fell off the back of the wagon...

She knew she wouldn't do it, but the thought made her smile nonetheless.

Mark looked at her suspiciously. "Why are you sm-"

He was cut off by a sudden shout.

7

The shout seemed to be coming from the far side of the wagon Jeremiah realized as he and the others raced toward the sound. They found Norman sitting on a small, folding stool with camera equipment all around him and a camera in his hands.

"What is it?" Jeremiah asked.

Norman looked up, watery blue eyes staring at him. "It's gone," he said.

"What's gone?" Kyle asked as he pushed his way through the growing crowd.

"Yesterday's footage. I was getting the equipment ready and I wanted to check the playback in a couple of spots, make sure the settings are working under these conditions, and I discovered that it was all gone. All of it's been erased."

"Are you sure the camera was working properly yesterday and it actually filmed something?" Jeremiah asked.

Norman glared at him. "Of course I'm sure. Besides, I checked it at lunch yesterday and then briefly last night as I was putting stuff away. I don't know how this could have happened."

"Could you have accidentally hit a button?" Traci asked. "I know once with my camera-"

"I am not an amateur or an imbecile!" Norman interrupted, pale cheeks flushing and voice raised in outrage. "I'm telling you this was no accident."

"But, who could possibly want to sabotage the footage?" Kyle asked, a blank look on his face.

Jeremiah knew that he for one wanted to sabotage the footage, but it seemed somebody else had beaten him to it. He glanced sideways at Hank and couldn't help but wonder if that's what the big man had been doing last night while everyone was supposed to be sleeping.

"This is a disaster!" Norman wailed and for a moment Jeremiah thought he was going to actually burst into tears.

Kyle seemed to rally at that. "Hey, it's all good, most of yesterday's footage will look a lot like today's footage. All we've lost is the start up."

"And the runaway horse," Norman pointed out.

Kyle sighed. "Is the footage from the helmet cameras secure? Hopefully we can just pull from those to get anything we need."

"I haven't checked yet," Norman said.

"Well, why don't you do that while we finish getting ready," Kyle suggested.

Norman sniffed and nodded.

"Chow in ten minutes!" Brent called from the front of the wagon.

"Alright, let's get this done," Kyle said, addressing the group who quickly began to disperse.

Jeremiah half-turned, ready to double check his sleeping bag and his backpack once more before bringing them over for loading into the wagon for the day.

"It will be okay," Liz said sympathetically, dropping her hand onto Norman's shoulder.

Norman looked up at her, adoration in his eyes. She let her hand linger a beat, two, and finally pulled it away.

Norman dropped his eyes back to his equipment and reached for the first helmet camera.

"Everything okay?" Cindy asked Jeremiah.

"Yeah," he said, turning to her.

They began to walk back to the sleeping area. She was limping, but moving better than he would have expected given how badly her ankle had been twisted. She was a fighter, whether she realized it or not. He thought of the discoloration already appearing around Kyle's eye and couldn't help but smirk. He couldn't have done better himself.

Of course, the rabbi part of him should gently remind her that violence wasn't the answer, especially when dealing with relatives. But he'd wanted to hit Kyle the moment he'd met him so it would be more than a little hypocritical of him. It was clear, though, that Kyle had pushed a very big button with her. From what he could tell it had something to do with their dead sister.

When they got back to civilization maybe it was time to have a talk with Cindy about Lisa. Actually opening up and talking about it might help her deal with her feelings about it a lot better. Most people had one or two topics that were taboo, that even bringing up could trigger strong emotional outbursts. Instead of suppressing that pain it needed to be explored and then released. Maybe he could help Cindy do that.

Back at the sleeping area Cindy set about rolling up her sleeping bag while he checked his backpack one last time. After the fiasco at the kid's camp earlier in the year he had allowed himself to pack what he considered the bare essentials and not just what he had been told to bring. So, in addition to the required clothes and toiletries, he also had his Swiss army knife, some rope, a small but well-stocked first aid kit, a compass, waterproof matches, fishing line and hook, a few heating packs, some nutrition bars, and finally a wicked looking survival knife that he kept buried at the bottom of the bag. He had refused to be unprepared this time for any contingency.

Next to him Cindy was trying for the third time to roll the sleeping bag tight enough that her ties would fit around it. He suppressed a smile as he watched her kneeling on it and straining to keep it as small as possible as she rolled it. She clearly was not used to them.

"Do much camping as a kid?" he asked, trying to make a joke.

She looked at him, her eyes suddenly haunted. "Once," she whispered.

He was taken aback by the raw pain on her face. He couldn't help but wonder if he had inadvertently touched on something to do with her sister.

"So, not a lot of slumber parties or church sleepovers?" he asked, trying to change the subject.

She shook her head.

"Would you like help rolling it up?"

From the way she bit her lip he could tell that she wanted to say yes, but felt like she should probably do it on her own.

"Here, this can't be helping your ankle. I'll take care of it," he said, quickly moving to take the decision away from her.

"Thank you," she said, relief flooding her voice.

She turned and busied herself with her own backpack while Jeremiah got to work rolling her sleeping bag. When he was finished thirty seconds later she stared at him.

"How did you do that?"

"Practice," he admitted.

"Show me how to do it that fast."

"Okay, tomorrow morning I'll help you do it, fair?"

"Fair," she agreed.

They heard the clanging of a metal triangle, the official call to breakfast.

"It's about time," Mark said, walking up with Traci. "I'm starving."

They grabbed plates of hot, delicious smelling food, and sat on the ground a ways away from everyone else.

"So, Traci," Mark said, around a mouthful of bacon. "I thought today would be your golden opportunity to talk some with Kyle and find out more about him. I know you love his shows. This could be your one chance to really find out all the behind-the-scenes stuff that noone ever gets to hear about."

He was trying to sound nonchalant, but Jeremiah watched as the two women exchanged a quick glance and then turned to look at Mark, eyebrows raised.

"What?" he asked.

"You think someone killed Martin, too. Admit it!" Traci said with a note of triumph in her voice.

"What? I never said...wait, 'too'? So, you ladies have come to the same conclusion?"

"Last night," Cindy confirmed. "We don't know if someone had a grudge against him or what."

"We went a step further," Jeremiah admitted. "Given what happened to your horse, we were thinking that it's possible someone is trying to sabotage the show or possibly even hurt Kyle."

"You think whoever killed Martin was really after Kyle?" Cindy asked, eyes round.

"We don't know, but everything that's happened so far seems very suspicious to us," Jeremiah said.

Mark shook his head. "Okay, next midnight confab we're all invited."

"I'm going to hold you to that," Traci said fervently.

Jeremiah tried to hide a smile. All of them had wanted Traci to have a fun and adventurous vacation. The prospect of a killer on the loose wasn't dampening her spirits in the least. If anything, she seemed even more energized. It made sense, in a way. Unlike the rest of them she never got to be the one solving the mystery. After years as a cop's wife now it was her turn and she seemed more than ready for the challenge.

"Okay then," Jeremiah said. "Today the name of the game is information. We need to find out as much as we can about everyone here. In addition to talking up some of the others I, for one, am going to be keeping a close eye on Hank. We still don't know what he was doing out of his sleeping bag last night."

"Good idea," Mark said. "If the answer is that he was just going to the little boy's tree, I'm going to be very disappointed."

Traci cheerfully socked him in the arm for that one.

Unfazed Mark continued, "Hopefully by dinner time we can begin to narrow our suspect list down a little bit. Traci, while you're questioning Kyle, keep a sharp look out to see if there's anyone interacting with him in an odd way."

She nodded eagerly.

"When we stop for lunch we should also mingle with some of the others. It would be a good time to talk, get to know them better," Jeremiah suggested.

"Good idea," Cindy said.

"Yeah, if we start acting friendlier and like less of a little clique it will make people less suspicious and help them open up," Mark noted. "Okay, let's keep a sharp eye out for anything suspicious and alert each other if we think we're onto something."

"Agreed," Cindy said.

They finished their breakfast, and returned their trays to the table by the wagon. Brent was already busy cleaning up and Jeremiah noticed that he gave Cindy a huge smile.

He felt his spine stiffen. A moment later he realized his lips were curling, as though he was baring his teeth at the man. He shook his head and turned aside, telling himself he had other things to focus on at the moment.

Everyone else was finishing up, too, and a moment later everyone was congregating around Norman and Kyle who were holding some of the helmets.

"How did the helmet cameras fare?" Kyle asked Norman just as Jeremiah walked up.

"Fine, except for one. It didn't capture any footage at all. I'm not sure if it malfunctioned or it just wasn't turned on," Norman said.

"Whose was it?" Kyle asked.

"Jeremiah's."

Kyle turned to Jeremiah with a frown. "You turned it on like I showed you, right?"

"Yes," Jeremiah lied.

"Huh. That's a shame, too. You were pretty close to Cindy when she fell off that horse, weren't you?"

"Pretty close," Jeremiah said without admitting how close.

"Well, let's try the camera again today. I'll make sure it's on before we head out."

Jeremiah nodded fighting back irritation at the implication that he wasn't able to turn a simple camera on properly. At least the one on his helmet was only showing what he saw and not his face. Still, he'd have to remember to turn it off again before he started talking to anyone, just as a precaution. He still planned to sabotage all the cameras anyway, but one could never be too safe.

After about another fifteen minutes of preparation everything was loaded into the chuck wagon. Helmets were distributed and Kyle made a great show of making sure Jeremiah had properly turned on his camera. Jeremiah grit his teeth through the entire process. The cowboys brought the horses up and Jeremiah helped Cindy up onto her seat on the wagon bench before mounting and riding off.

Traci waved to him before trotting her horse after Kyle's. He had a feeling she would be sticking to him like glue all day. He turned away and his eyes zeroed in on Hank.

In addition to the helmet cams everyone else was wearing, Hank also had a camera rig strapped to his left shoulder. He rode with reins in his left hand, leaving his right hand free to adjust the camera when he felt the need.

It would have been easy for him to sabotage the footage while he was up in the middle of the night. The question was why? He hadn't even been part of the original crew, but a last minute replacement. What could he possibly have to gain by hurting Kyle or the production?

Jeremiah urged his horse forward. He had his work cut out for him today. In addition to questioning as many people as he could, he still had to act like he was trying to herd the cattle. Fortunately, multi-tasking came easily to him. Also fortunately, nobody was going to expect great things out of him since noone knew how well he rode. He had been fortunate in that he was pretty sure nobody had seen how he had pulled Cindy off her horse. Although thanks to Mark's comment the night before he'd have to remember to act a little more stiff and sore tonight after dismounting.

It was just one more thing to think about, to juggle. This trip was turning out to be more work and more stress than he could have ever dreamed.

Cindy was more than a little unsettled by the thought that someone might be out to hurt her brother. The more she thought about it, though, the more it made snese. Cindy's job that morning was to question Brent. Almost two hours into the morning drive she got her opportunity.

"That sure is going to be a beautiful black eye Kyle will have in another day or so," Brent said out of the blue as Kyle trotted by on his horse. He had been talking about his plans for food for the rest of the trip and how Kyle had thrown him the curveball of wanting it to seem like authentic grub while still being Kosher.

"Sometimes Kyle can just get under a person's skin, you know?"

He chuckled. "Apparently he got under yours."

It was not the response she had been hoping for so she pushed a little harder. "Sometimes I think it's me, that everyone else in the world thinks he's a saint. I know my parents do. Maybe I am the crazy one."

"I don't think everyone sees him as the golden boy he thinks of himself as," Brent replied.

"Really?" Cindy asked.

"Really. Now, this is my first time working with him, but it's not that big a network and you hear things sometimes."

"Like what?" she asked, not having to fake the eagerness in her voice.

"I know poor Martin didn't want to work on this show. He disliked working with Kyle because Kyle thinks of himself as the director and cinematographer of his shows instead of just the star."

"Then why did Martin agree to work on the show?"

"He didn't have a lot of choice, the way I heard it. Kyle pitched a fit because he wanted the best cinematographer on the job. Such a tragedy, too, that it got Martin killed, especially when Norman would have loved to have been here in the first place."

Cindy blinked, trying to hide her rising excitement. "Norman wanted to be the cinematographer for the show?"

"He was supposed to be. In fact, the idea for the show was actually his. He was so excited when the network decided to run with it. And it broke his heart when the executives told him he wouldn't be working on it. We were filming an episode of my show the day he got the news. I'll never forget it. I can't remember ever seeing anyone so torn up about something in my life. I ended up convincing everyone to take the rest of the day off. He was no good to anybody in that condition."

"Wow, he must hate Kyle," Cindy muttered.

Her mind was racing. It sounded like Norman also had reason to hate Martin. But Norman hadn't been there the night Martin was killed. He had arrived really early the next morning, though, suggesting that wherever he had been couldn't have been too far away.

"You know, I could hold Kyle down while Norman punched his other eye," Cindy joked, hoping to cover her intense interest in the information she was getting.

Brent laughed. "That would be a sight! Norman isn't the type, though. He wouldn't hurt a fly."

"So, I guess I'll just have to pin Kyle anyway and see if anyone else volunteers to blacken his other eye. That way he can at least have a matched set."

Brent shook his head. "He really must have pissed you off."

"You have no idea," she said fervently.

"You never know. Roddy might take you up on the offer. I know he gets really frustrated sometimes. He's supposed to be a production assistant but Kyle treats him like his personal assistant. Or maybe Wayne would take you up on it. I heard he took a swing at Kyle over something when they were filming in Belize last year. Never heard what happened."

It seemed the list of people who might want to hurt her brother just kept growing and growing.

"At this rate maybe I'll auction off the privilege," she said.

Brent laughed again. "I'll bid a dollar. After all, making bacon out of lamb isn't nearly the hardest thing I'm having to do this week."

"What is?" she asked.

"I had to learn how to drive this wagon," he said. "And I'm afraid of horses."

The way he said it made Cindy laugh. She couldn't help herself.

"Wait, make it two dollars. I nearly forgot that I have to make his dinner separate from everyone else's."

"Why?"

"Apparently the Kosher stew I came up with for everyone else isn't good enough for him. He wants pork in his. I swear that man would put pork in anything. Plus, he's obsessed with this particular type of truffle salt. He wants it in everything. Well, he can have it in his stew, but I refuse to put it in anything else. If I'm going to use truffles I want the real thing, you know?"

"And I thought he was high maintenance when we were kids," she joked.

He laughed as well.

"Okay, so the bidding is at two dollars. I'll have to see if I can get that up a few more dollars when we stop for lunch," she said.

"Oh, I'm sure you'll have some takers on that," he said with a laugh.

"Yeah, who do you think would pay top dollar to slug my brother?" she asked.

He turned and looked at her, and she suddenly noticed just how intensely green his eyes were. He had been smiling a moment before but now his face began to change, becoming more serious, more intense.

"You know, you ask a lot of questions," he said.

She caught her breath. She had pushed too far and made him suspicious. She felt panic begin to flare up inside her and she tried to calm herself down. After all, that would only matter if he turned out to be the killer.

"What can I say?" she asked, sounding more than a little breathless. "I'm just naturally curious."

"I kind of got that impression. I think I know what your game is, though."

"You do?" she asked, trying to hide the panic she was feeling.

"Yes. And I have a question for you."

"A question for me? What kind of question?"

He leaned closer until his face was all she could see. His eyes were blazing and they pinned her to the spot.

"Let's just say someone's life hinges on how you answer."

8

Cindy thought about screaming for help, but her throat constricted. "What is the question?" she barely managed to whisper.

"Will you go out with me?"

She stared at him, sure that she was going insane. There was no way she could have heard him right. "What?" she gasped at last.

"See, not the right answer. The answer is 'yes, I'd love to go out with you'," he said.

"You're asking me out on a date?"

"Yes, I am," he said, still intense.

"How does someone's life hinge on that answer?" she asked, blinking rapidly in her relief and confusion.

"Because my life is going to be over if you say no."

"I-I. Okay," she blurted out, still too rattled to really grasp what was happening.

"Excellent!" he said, smiling and leaning back. "I promise you, you won't regret it."

Cindy had no idea what to say. Fortunately that seemed to be okay with Brent and they rode for a while in silence.

After a while Zack rode up beside the wagon. "I didn't get a chance to ask you how your ankle was doing this morning," he said.

"Much better. Thank you," she answered.

"Glad to hear it. You can probably return to a horse tomorrow if you want." He gave a shrewd look. "Or, if you need me to, I can order you to ride in the wagon for the rest of the trip," he said.

She smiled. "I appreciate that. I'm leaning toward the wagon, but let me see how I feel in the morning."

The truth was, there wouldn't have been any question for her if it hadn't been for Brent asking her out. Now she felt a bit shy and awkward around him and it might be just enough to get her back on a horse. At least she wanted to keep her options open.

Next Zack addressed Brent. "We've been making better time than expected this morning. We'll be stopping in an about an hour, there's a little draw with some good grass and a stream just over the next hill."

"Sounds good," Brent said.

Zack tipped his hat and then headed back for the herd.

Brent urged the horses to a faster clip. "I'd like to start setting up before the rest get there," he explained.

"Before the hungry hoard descends?" she asked.

"You've got that right. The camp cook thing is an awkward setup because it doesn't allow you enough time to really prepare the food before everyone's ready to eat it."

"I can imagine that would be hard."

"It is. But, like I always say, 'Where a good chef falls, a great chef rises to the challenge.'"

"I like that," she said.

"Thanks. I came up with it myself the day I taped my first cooking show. I kept thinking I wanted some sort of inspirational catch phrase and that was what I came up with."

"It's good, and it could apply to more areas of work and life."

"I know, right? Substitute another word for chef like man or woman or cowboy and it works just as well."

They fell back into silence and Cindy was surprised at how soon they reached the location Zack had described. Since they had beaten everyone else she volunteered to help and was soon busy making sandwiches. She had just finished when she saw the herd crest the rise.

Jeremiah was toward the front of the herd and she stopped for a moment, marveling at how well he rode. He looked so natural and graceful. It made her almost want to give riding another try even though she knew she could never achieve his level of skill.

As he rode toward her she continued to stare. He seemed larger than life, invincible, like some sort of knight in shining armor. She felt herself relax ever so slightly the closer he got, and with a start she realized that having him around always made her feel safer.

My hero, she thought, and then felt herself blush.

Jeremiah felt a surge of relief as he saw Cindy standing beside the chuck wagon. He'd been unhappy when it had gone on ahead and realized he'd been worrying about her. Given everything that had happened to her, he was always far more comfortable when she was where he could see her at all times.

A few minutes later he was off his horse and walking over with Mark and Traci. After momentarily forgetting, he forced himself to walk a little stiffly as if the riding was getting to him.

Cindy looked pale and slightly uneasy and it worried him. The others must have noticed, too.

"What happened to you?" Traci asked before he could say anything.

"Brent asked me on a date," Cindy blurted out.

It was all he could do not to say something he'd regret.

"Well that was unexpected," Traci said.

"Tell me about it."

"What did you say?"

"I was so shocked, I'm pretty sure I said 'yes'," Cindy admitted.

"Really?" Traci asked, managing to look even more surprised.

"Apparently so. He totally caught me off guard. He was saying that I was asking a bunch of questions and then he said he had one and I actually thought he was threatening me and then...he wasn't."

"Well, at least that will make a great story for your kids if he ends up being the one."

Cindy groaned.

Traci just smirked at her.

Jeremiah felt like he wanted to rip something apart with his bare hands. A number of objects and people kept flashing through his mind as he clenched his fists, chief among them Brent.

You have no right to feel this way, he told himself sternly.

It didn't help ease the tightness in his chest, though.

"Okay, let's break it up. Remember, it's lunchtime. We're supposed to be mingling," Mark said.

Mark was grateful that the other three listened and did as he said. Cindy headed over to talk to Liz while Jeremiah made his way toward the cowboys. He was personally planning on having a chat with Wayne and Junior. Divide and conquer was their best strategy here.

More than anything else, though, he had wanted to get Jeremiah thinking about something other than Brent asking Cindy out. He had no idea if either Traci or Cindy had noticed but there had been a murderous look on Jeremiah's face when he found out. It had been so intense that it had actually scared Mark. Apparently the one thing that angered the rabbi more than someone trying to kill Cindy was someone trying to date Cindy.

Good to know.

Jeremiah grabbed his food and took a seat on the ground with Zack and Curly who both looked at him in surprise. Tex must be the one in charge of taking care of the horses and watching thc cattlc whilc they ate, he realized.

"I just wanted to thank you both for the great job you're doing," Jeremiah said by means of explaining his sitting down with them.

"Just doing our job," Curly said.

Zack rolled his eyes at the other cowboy. "You're welcome seems like an appropriate response."

Jeremiah smiled.

"You ride pretty well," Zack said. "You grow up with horses?"

"Something like that," Jeremiah admitted. "I enjoy riding."

"Yeah, me, too. I missed that more than anything when I was deployed overseas," Zack said.

"I understand. Army life is hard," Jeremiah said.

"You served?" Zack asked.

Jeremiah nodded. "I was born and raised in Israel. There, everyone serves their time."

Zack shook his head. "That's one way of doing it. I don't know if I could stand that, though. Someday I'd like to have kids and I plan on steering them clear away from that particular experience."

His eyes looked haunted as he spoke. Jeremiah realized that the doctor turned cowboy had seen far more overseas than he ever wanted to. He'd seen enough that he abandoned medicine in favor of something more isolated and less bloody. Jeremiah had seen a lot of men go through similar transformations.

"You grew up in Israel?" Curly asked, suddenly seeming interested.

"Yes, why?"

"My girlfriend is Jewish. She keeps talking about taking a trip there."

"I would recommend it, especially if she wants to really connect with the culture and the people," Jeremiah said.

"Mind if I ask you some questions?"

"Go right ahead."

Cindy went and sat down on the ground next to Liz with her food. "How's it going?" she asked.

"Good. One of the strangest shoots I've ever been on, but good."

"How's it strange?" Cindy asked.

"With all the dust and everything else and the constant movement and the fact that my kit has to ride in the wagon I'm not checking makeup and doing touchups every so often. I feel like I've got almost nothing to do and I keep feeling bad like I'm shirking my duties, but that's the nature of the beast, I guess."

"It's funny, I never think of Kyle wearing makeup," Cindy said.

"Oh, trust me, lots and lots on most shooting days," Liz said with a smile. "But, that's being an actor. It's going to take a lot to cover that shiner he's working on. Then with all the environmental factors I'm not even sure how well I'm going to be able to disguise it."

"Sorry, I didn't realize I was going to be making your job hard," Cindy said.

"I'm sure all you were thinking about at the time was how much you wanted to hit him," Liz said.

"Yup. I'm thinking of auctioning off the chance to black his other eye. Who do you think will bid the most?"

Liz shook her head. "Who knows? Kyle's a bit of an egomaniac, but no more so than most stars. Most of the time he's a lot nicer, too."

"I can't be the only one who wants to deck him," Cindy said, working to put the disappointment in her voice.

Liz shrugged. "Personally I'd rather smack Junior. The little perv keeps hitting on me."

"Not your type I take it."

"No way," Liz said fervently. "Besides, I've got a boyfriend."

"That must be nice."

"It is," Liz said, breaking out into a grin. "He's perfect. Kind, thoughtful, brilliant."

Cindy felt her own thoughts drifting toward Jeremiah and it took all her self control not to turn and look for him.

"How about you, dating anyone?" Liz asked.

"No," Cindy said quickly.

"Are you sure?" Liz asked.

Cindy nodded.

"Don't worry. You'll find Mr. Right. And when you do, it will be magic. You'll do anything for him and follow wherever he goes."

Cindy forced herself to smile.

Mark ate lunch with Wayne and Junior who weren't very talkative. When it was over he had his work cut out for him just staying on his horse and paying attention to the terrain and cattle to try and get close enough to anyone to question them.

The cattle were moving slower than they had in the morning and Mark felt like he ate a ton of dust. He was certain he was never going to get the stink of the cattle out of his skin and hair let alone his sinus passages. He got occasional glimpses of Traci and she was usually grinning from ear to ear. He had to admire her chipper attitude and wished he could share it.

His spine was beginning to feel like it had been jolted one too many times when they finally reached the place where they were going to be spending the night. He felt relief surge through him. He'd been afraid he was going to fall off his horse from pure exhaustion before they made it.

Two of the cowboys bunched up the cattle while the rest of the group clustered around Kyle. Kyle's face was smeared with dirt and dust from the trail and Mark couldn't help but wonder if he looked better or worse.

"Nice job today everyone," Kyle said. "Make sure to drop your helmets off behind the chuck wagon. Set up camp. Dinner I'm told will be in half an hour."

Mark practically fell off his horse, wondering how he was going to survive another four days of this. Traci groaned as she slid off her horse and tossed the reins to Tex. Even Jeremiah looked a little stiff as he dismounted which definitely made Mark feel better.

They moved to the back of the chuck wagon where Cindy had already pulled out their sleeping bags and backpacks. After dumping their helmets in a pile for the camera guys, the four of them took their gear and headed over to the spot where Kyle had indicated they should set up camp.

Mark tried to squat down on the ground and instead landed on his rump. Traci snickered and he just shook his head. "This is hard work. I vote that Cindy gets to set everything up since she got to ride on the wagon."

"I was injured, remember?" Cindy said, blinking big doe eyes.

It was so funny he laughed despite his exhaustion.

"Well, I found out some interesting things today," Traci said, lowering her voice. "Apparently this show is going to be their flagship for the new season."

Jeremiah frowned. "You think this could be more about hurting the network than Kyle?"

"I don't know," she said. "I do know that he and Wayne aren't very fond of each other."

"I heard Wayne took a swing at him while they were filming in Belize," Cindy said.

"I heard that, too, but I didn't hear what provoked it," Mark said.

"Me either," Cindy admitted. "I also heard that Roddy is sick of being treated like Kyle's personal assistant."

"Interesting," Mark said, stroking his chin and electing to stay seated for a few more minutes. The muscles in his thighs were twitching painfully.

"I talked to both Zack and Curly. They seemed like nice guys and neither of them had ever worked with Kyle or anyone from the Escape! Channel for that matter. Curly had never even heard of it. I never had a chance to talk with Tex, though," Jeremiah said. "Hank was singularly unforthcoming," he added.

"You mean more than you?" Mark quipped.

He got a glare for his troubles.

"Apparently this show was all Norman's idea," Cindy said.

"The new cinematographer?" Mark asked. "How does that work?"

"I guess he pitched the show, the network loved it, but they wanted Martin because he was the better cinematographer."

Mark whistled. "That's cause for some resentment right there."

"Apparently he was filming one of Brent's shows the day they broke the news to him and he took it hard."

"Who wouldn't?" Mark asked, noticing that a muscle in Jeremiah's jaw was beginning to twitch. "I mean, you have this thing, you think it's yours, and then someone else takes it away from you."

The muscle in Jeremiah's jaw twitched more.

Don't push him, Mark lectured himself. He shouldn't have made that last dig. He wasn't even sure why he had except maybe to get the rabbi's goat.

Traci glanced sideways at him then changed the subject. "I did get one other thing out of Kyle. Apparently he and

Liz went on like one date which was fairly disastrous. She ended up telling him he just wasn't her type, but that was like two years ago and they've still been working together without any problems."

"Interesting, Liz didn't mention anything about that to me," Cindy said.

"Maybe it wasn't a big deal to her," Mark suggested.

"Or she was embarrassed to admit she dated your brother and dumped him," Traci said.

Mark sighed. "So, do you think of our ten suspects there's anyone we can safely rule out yet?"

There was a moment of silence. Finally Jeremiah spoke up. "My gut tells me we can rule out Zack and Curly. I don't think either of them had anything to do with it."

"Okay, let's move them onto the Probably Not But Don't Turn Your Back On Them Anyway list," Mark said. "That leaves us with eight people, seven of whom work for the network. We have to find a way to chop that list down further."

They heard the ringing of the triangle that signified that dinner was ready. They all stood up just as Kyle jogged over.

"Cind, got a sec?" he asked.

"Sure," she said, taking a deep breath. "Go ahead," she told the others.

In a moment she was alone with her brother. His eye had really turned black from where she had hit him and inwardly she winced.

"I'm sorry about that," she said. "I shouldn't have hit you."

Kyle grinned. "Don't worry about it. I've been hit by way angrier, way stronger people than you."

She smiled back, surprised that he could have such a sense of humor about it. "I didn't think anyone could get angrier than that."

"Trust me they can, and with far less provocation. I try to live life every moment to the fullest and sometimes my way of doing things rubs people the wrong way. I don't know how to be any different, though."

"So, you're girlfriend."

"Lisa," he said cautiously.

"Lisa. Do you have a picture of her?"

His eyes lit up at that. "I do." He dug out his phone. "I don't know why I haven't just stowed this in my gear. We're not going to get any reception until we make town," he said.

"Habit?" she suggested.

"Probably. Battery's about gone anyway. Here you go," he said, handing it to her at last.

Cindy stared at the girl with long, dark brown hair and large grey eyes. She was smiling at the camera and she was strikingly beautiful.

"She's gorgeous," Cindy said, handing the phone back.

"I think so," Kyle said, turning the phone off and returning it to his pocket. "I'm still not sure how I got so lucky."

He sounded completely sincere and it surprised Cindy. She always thought of her brother as the one with the super ego.

"Hopefully I can meet her sometime soon."

"We'll be at Mom and Dad's for Thanksgiving again this year."

"Not that soon," Cindy said, forcing a smile.

"Can't blame a guy for trying. They miss you, you know."

"Who?"

"Mom and Dad, that's who."

Cindy dropped her eyes. "I'm sure as long as you're there they're just fine."

"Look, I know Mom can be a bit...obsessive over my career."

"Obsessive?" Cindy asked with a bitter laugh. "That's a bit of an understatement."

"I just think she's living vicariously through me or something. I think she wishes she was out there having more adventures."

Cindy wondered briefly if that could be true.

Kyle sighed. "Look, I don't want to get all family psycho-analyzy here."

"Good word."

"Thanks, made it up just now. Anyway, I just wanted to make sure we were okay."

She nodded. "We're good."

"That's a relief. Because I heard a rumor you were auctioning off the opportunity to blacken my other eye."

She laughed, startled. "How did you hear that?"

"I have my sources. Now, let's go get some food."

They walked over together. Everyone else was busy eating. Jeremiah looked at her and raised a questioning eyebrow. She flashed him a nod and a smile to let him know that everything was okay, at least for the moment.

There was a big pot of stew on the rough table set up behind the chuck wagon and one remaining bowl for Cindy.

"Hey, Cookie, where's my food?" Kyle called jovially.

Brent stepped down from the back of the wagon, a bowl in his hand. Cindy took one look at him and stepped forward. He was pasty white and he was sweating profusely.

"Brent, are you okay?" Cindy asked.

"Something's not right," the chef gasped. The bowl slipped from his fingers, spilling its contents all over the ground. Then he made a horrific groaning sound, clutched his stomach, and collapsed forward, slamming into her.

9

Cindy's injured ankle gave way beneath her and she and Brent both tumbled to the ground. She landed hard on her hip and shoulder and the weight of Brent on top of her pushed her onto her back. She writhed in pain as she felt like her ribcage was being crushed and she tried to push him off.

A moment later strong hands were rolling him off her and she scrambled away, hands and feet digging into the earth as she tried to put some distance between herself and the body, because she was almost certain Brent was dead.

"What happened?" she managed to gasp even though she was still in agonizing pain.

No one answered her. No one even looked at her. Everyone was instead crowded around Brent. More people rushed over, blocking her view of Brent and what was going on.

"Brent! Brent! What's wrong?" she heard Kyle shouting.

"He's not moving!" she heard Liz exclaim.

"He's not breathing either," Mark said, his voice much calmer than the others.

"Where's the doctor? Somebody get the doctor," Kyle said. "Roddy, go find Zack!"

A moment later Roddy rushed by her, tripping over her in his haste. He landed sprawled on the ground as Cindy gasped and grabbed at her bad ankle hoping he hadn't just broken it.

"Roddy, hurry!" Kyle shouted.

Roddy picked himself up with a curse and raced on.

"Everyone move back, give me some room," Jeremiah said.

Nobody moved.

"Okay, people, you heard him. Everyone back away!" Mark said, voice raised, authority dripping from every syllable.

Everyone shuffled backward a few steps and through a gap she could now see Brent laying on his back, unmoving. Jeremiah was leaning over him and he was doing continuous chest compressions.

She put a shaking hand over her mouth. Just a few minutes before Brent had been so animated, laughing, smiling at her. Now he was just a body on the ground growing cold, an empty shell.

She heard running footsteps behind her and turned to see Zack racing up to her. He took one look at her and hesitated.

"Are you-"

"Not me, Brent," she interrupted pointing at the body.

He nodded and pushed his way through the people crowding around. "What happened?"

"He collapsed," Mark said.

"He has no pulse," Jeremiah added as he continued with the chest compressions.

"Heart attack?" Zack asked.

"Didn't look like it to me," Jeremiah said.

"I thought at first that he had food poisoning. He was sweating heavily, pale, and looked like he was having stomach cramps right before he collapsed," Mark added.

"What do you think happened?" Kyle asked as Zack began checking Brent over while Jeremiah continued to administer chest compressions.

"Isn't is obvious?" Cindy burst out before she could stop herself.

All eyes swiveled to her.

"He was poisoned," she added. "And not just something accidental like food poisoning. He was murdered."

Cindy's voice sounded off, that was the first thing that Jeremiah noticed. The second was that she was broadcasting her theory to everyone. Usually she was a lot more circumspect. He'd be willing to bet she was in shock. It was possible that she was also injured from the fall. He'd have to check on her and have the doctor look her over, too, as soon as possible.

He glanced up at Mark who was grimacing, clearly also not happy that she was letting everyone know what she suspected. Traci quickly turned and hurried over to Cindy, clearly making a show of fussing over her.

"Are you okay, Cindy? That was a really bad fall. Did you reinjure your ankle?"

"Yes."

"That must hurt an awful lot. Did you hit your head? I'll see if I can find a blanket. I think you're going into shock."

"I am not going into shock!" Cindy said, even though it was clear to Jeremiah that she was.

Even Kyle was starting to look more than a little concerned. He took a couple of halting steps toward her. When he spoke his voice was very patronizing, as though he was talking to a child. "Cind, look, I know that this is a terrible, terrible tragedy-"

"Don't talk to me like that!" she snapped. "You of all people have no right to talk to me like that. You are such an idiot, a blind, stupid idiot. Don't you know what's going on here?"

Jeremiah winced as he realized what was coming next. It was like watching a train wreck, complete with that terrible sinking sensation in your stomach and the knowledge that there was nothing you could do to stop it.

"I know that you're upset. I know that you liked Brent and now...something has happened to him."

"That's not it at all," Cindy ground out.

She struggled to her feet and it was painful to watch. She was nearly up when she almost collapsed and Jeremiah flinched then relaxed as she managed to keep her footing. She stood at last, the toes of her bad ankle barely scraping the ground. She was dirty, disheveled, and weaving back and forth. Her lips were quivering and her eyes were blazing. Yet somehow she had never looked more beautiful to him as she stood there, righteous anger clothing her.

"What's going on here Kyle is that Martin, Brent, the snake, the breaking saddle strap, none of these things were accidents."

"What do you mean?" he asked, his face growing pale.

"What I mean is, someone is trying to kill you and you're too stupid to realize it."

There was a moment of absolute shocked silence and then pandemonium erupted as everyone started talking at once.

"What are you talking about?" Kyle demanded.

Cindy could barely hear him above all the others who were suddenly shouting and demanding answers.

"These things weren't accidents. Someone killed Martin, mistaking him for you in the dark. Then they tried to sabotage your saddle, but we had switched horses so I was hurt instead. Now whoever it is has killed Brent."

"You're crazy!" Kyle said, coming to stand right next to her and waving his hand to try to get everyone else to be quiet. It did no good, if anything the din just got louder.

"Am I? Which one of us has the experience solving murders? Huh? You? No, that's right. I think it's me. Listen to me. I know what I'm talking about. And I'm not the only one that thinks that's what's going on. Mark, Traci, and Jeremiah think so, too."

"I don't care what they think."

"You should care. Mark is a homicide detective. You should listen to him if you won't listen to me."

"These are accidents, terrible, unfortunate accidents, but that's it."

"Why won't you see the truth?" she demanded, frustration and fear welling inside her.

"You really think someone would go to all these lengths to hurt the show?" he asked.

"No, not the show, you!"

"But, how does Brent getting food poisoning factor into that?"

"Don't you see? Almost everyone else got a chance to eat dinner while you and I were talking. They're fine. It can't be food poisoning or they'd be dropping, too. And, last I checked, even extreme food poisoning bad enough to be fatal would take a lot longer to kill you. This was actual poisoning."

"But, why would someone want to poison Brent?" he asked, bewilderment on his face.

"They wouldn't. That's what I've been saying. They weren't trying to kill him, they were trying to kill you."

"I don't see how."

"Kyle, you were having a different dinner than everyone else. Someone poisoned your dinner. What they didn't count on was the fact that Brent probably tasted your food before serving it. Isn't that what chefs do?"

"But how could they poison my food? That would have meant someone had to be there while he was preparing it. Wouldn't he have seen them?"

"Not if they did it ahead of time," Mark chimed in.

"But, how?"

That's when it struck Cindy. "The salt."

"What?" Kyle asked.

"Your special truffle salt. He refused to use it on anyone's food but yours. How many other people knew that you ate that salt, that you had to have it?"

Kyle blinked at her. "I-I don't know," he said finally. "No one. Everyone. I don't know."

"Think, Kyle," Mark said.

"Everyone knows he eats that bloody salt," Wayne growled suddenly.

Cindy glanced briefly at him. She'd been working hard to tune the others out, but that came through loud and clear.

"So, anyone could have poisoned the salt and inadvertently killed Brent," she said.

Zack put his hand on Jeremiah's shoulder and he turned and looked at the doctor. Zack's eyes were clouded and he shook his head grimly. "It's okay. You can stop now. He's gone."

Jeremiah looked down at Brent's body. The entire time he had been continuing to do chest compressions though he had ceased being aware of it. He stopped and then a moment later lifted his hands off the dead man's chest.

"You did all you could, no one could have done more," Zack said.

Jeremiah nodded.

The drama was continuing to play out a few feet away, but for the moment he had no wish to wade into the fray. His arm muscles were throbbing from the speed and number of compressions he had done.

He looked down at Brent. The man had been poisoned. He had no doubts about that. He just wished Cindy had waited to share her theories until someone other than him said so.

He looked up and met Zack's eyes.

"He was poisoned," Zack said, the words half statement, half question as though he already knew the answer but he needed someone else to confirm it for him.

"Yes, I think so," Jeremiah said quietly.

"I've only seen half a dozen real poisoning cases, all but one of them self-inflicted," Zack said.

"I don't think he did this to himself," Jeremiah said.

Zack shook his head. "He was the cook, he was the one with the best access to the food. We should warn the others," he said, alarm beginning to register on his face.

Jeremiah shook his head. "It can't be in the stew. Most of us have already eaten that and there have been no ill effects yet."

"Then what?"

"Something he ate that the rest of us didn't. It has to be."

"So, we need to figure out what that is and isolate it fast."

"He was just carrying Kyle's meal out from the wagon when he collapsed. It went all over the ground. Kyle wasn't eating out of the same pot as everyone else. Maybe there was something in that food that was different."

"So, Cindy's right, someone is trying to kill her brother?" Zack asked.

Jeremiah nodded. "I'm fairly certain."

"That's good enough for me. Let's go see if we can figure out what poisoned the chef."

They both stood up. Traci was just returning from the camp area with a blanket. Jeremiah waved at her and she diverted course from Cindy to him.

"Sorry," he said with a grimace as he took it from her.

She nodded, averting her eyes from the body on the ground.

Jeremiah laid the blanket over Brent. They'd have to deal with him more properly later, after they'd had a chance to sort a few things out.

The remains of Kyle's stew were on the ground just a couple of feet away. Jeremiah pointed to it and Zack squatted down beside it.

"To tell you the truth, I can't even begin to figure out what I should be looking for," the doctor said after a moment.

"It's something we should collect and quarantine so that it can be analyzed later," Jeremiah said.

"Got a plastic bag and something to scoop with?"

"I'll check the wagon."

Jeremiah climbed up into the back of the wagon. He moved over to a big ice chest and opened it up. Rows of packets of cut up portions of meat and other spoilable items met his eyes. He picked up a package of the bacon and noticed that it was double bagged. He removed the outer bag and replaced the bacon in the cooler before closing it back up.

Then he turned and pulled a large serving spoon out of a canvas case that held a variety of utensils. He carried the bag and spoon outside and hopped onto the ground.

"Shall I do the honors?" he asked.

"That's okay, I've got it," Zack said. He had a small black bag that had been with the remaining luggage outside the wagon beside him. He had pulled out a disposable pair of plastic gloves and was putting them on.

Once gloved he took the bag and spoon and carefully ladled what he could of the stew into the bag. At the last he sealed it with the spoon inside. Then he carefully piled a couple of inches of fresh dirt over the contaminated area and tamped it all down before removing the gloves and disposing of them in a small trash bag he also pulled out of the bag.

"Okay, now the big question is what to do with this?" he said, indicating the bag of stew.

It was the very question Jeremiah had been pondering. They needed to put it somewhere safe where it couldn't be sabotaged, stolen, inadvertently destroyed, or accidentally eaten. Keeping it with the medical supplies wasn't a good idea in case the bag was punctured and contaminated everything.

"Brent's bag, that's the only place I can think of and we put it in its own section of the wagon where we can isolate it from everyone else's things."

"Sounds like a good idea," Zack said.

Aside from the cowboys' gear, Brent's bag and sleeping bag were the only ones that hadn't been transferred to the campsite yet. Both were easy to find because he had luggage tags with his name on them.

Mark disengaged from the group that was still surrounding Cindy and joined them. "That's where you're storing the sample?" he asked skeptically after Jeremiah caught him up to speed.

"You have a better idea?" Jeremiah asked.

The detective shook his head.

"I'm going to stow this in the front of the wagon, just behind where Cindy is sitting."

"Okay. See if you can find a packet of truffle salt while you're at it. Apparently Kyle always uses it on everything and Cindy's convinced that might be what was poisoned.

Jeremiah put the poisoned food into the bag and then went and stuffed it into the far right hand corner of the wagon. He then put Brent's backpack on top of it for good measure, as one extra barrier between the sample and the rest of the things in the wagon.

He then began to look around for a bag of truffle salt. He assumed it would be fairly small. He found some other herbs the chef had clearly used, more food for the rest of the journey, and more cookware. Nowhere, though, could he find any truffle salt.

He closed his eyes, trying to picture the scene immediately after Brent had collapsed. It was possible that the killer could have snuck into the wagon and grabbed the salt. Unfortunately, where he'd been on the ground next to Brent, he'd had his back to the wagon. So had Mark.

When he exited he noticed that things seemed to be calming down slightly. He wasn't fooled, though. He figured everyone had just exhausted themselves and shock was starting to set in.

Wayne, Junior, Liz and Norman were standing a little ways off, huddled together, not saying anything, but just looking miserable. Hank was standing by himself, arms crossed over his chest, face unreadable. Cindy was sitting on the ground again and Traci was huddled beside her.

"I couldn't find it," Jeremiah said quietly to Mark.

"Well, it's not out here anywhere, I looked," Mark said.

"So, the killer must have grabbed it in the confusion after Brent collapsed. Any chance they still have it on them?"

"If it were me, I'd have gotten rid of it fast," Mark said. "Won't hurt us to look, though."

Kyle had turned and was looking all around him. A moment later he spotted Zack and walked over to him.

"Where's Roddy?" Kyle asked.

"I haven't seen him," Zack said.

"Didn't he come to get you when Brent collapsed?" Kyle asked, frowning.

"No. I finished unsaddling the horses and I was heading in to grab dinner, heard some shouting and saw people clustered around. I figured someone else had gotten hurt and I came running."

"So, where is Roddy?" Kyle asked, panic beginning to tinge his voice.

It was a good question. Jeremiah glanced around. He didn't see the man. He did, however, see Tex finally heading in from where he and Curly had been bedding down the cattle.

"What's been going on?" Tex asked as he walked up. His eyes fell on the blanket that was over Brent.

"The cook was killed," Zack said shortly.

Before Tex could say anything Kyle grabbed his shoulder. "Have you seen Roddy?"

"Not since lunch, why?"

Kyle blanched. "Okay, people, listen up!" he bellowed. "Roddy is missing. We need to break up into groups and go and search for him," he said.

Everyone turned to stare at him, their faces lined with concern but still dazed and shocked.

"This is what we're going to do. We're-"

"Okay, pretty boy you can sit down and stop talking now. You're not in charge anymore," Mark interrupted.

"What? Why?" Kyle asked.

"I'm in charge now, because this has officially become a crime scene."

10

Mark's cop instincts were kicking into high gear which was both a good and a bad thing, Jeremiah thought. It always made him a little nervous when Mark was in full detective mode. The man was smart and hyper-observant. Which meant that Jeremiah needed to be more careful.

"Hold on," Kyle started to say.

Mark gave him a withering glare. "You keep your mouth shut so that I don't decide to go ahead and let the killer take another crack at you. Understand?"

Kyle nodded mutely, eyes practically bulging out of his head. Jeremiah couldn't help but wonder how long it had been since someone had talked to him that way. At least the seriousness of the situation seemed to be finally sinking in and he had enough sense to do as Mark was telling him.

"Okay, first things first. I'm going to need each of you to turn out your pockets. *All* of them. Do not make me search you, because trust me I will and it would be better to just turn yourself in now."

"What are you looking for?" Traci asked.

"We're looking for a packet of truffle salt," Mark said. "Traci, Cindy, if you would be so good as to check out what everyone is holding and feel free to check their pockets, too, if you don't trust them. Go ahead and turn yours out first, so everyone can get a good look at them."

Traci pulled a hair scrunchie out of one pocket and a small tube of eye drops out of the other. Cindy pulled out some tissue and a couple of allergy pills.

"Very good," Mark said. "I have nothing in my pockets, but in the interest of disclosure, I am carrying this," Mark said. He untucked his shirt and pulled out a gun from the back of his waistband.

The others began to mutter. It was a bold move, also one that leveled the playing field a bit. All three of the cowboys wore guns. Now everyone else knew Mark did, too.

"Jeremiah, show what you've got," Mark said.

He dutifully complied, holding up a protein bar he'd had in his pocket since that morning. Given what had happened to Brent, he was already wishing he had brought more of them. Cindy and Lisa walked over to inspect it, but they didn't check his pockets. He was glad because he didn't want anyone to know that he was also carrying a very small Swiss army knife.

"Now, Kyle, if you'd be so kind."

Kyle looked like he wanted to object, but he pulled his phone out of his pocket along with a comb, a small mirror, what looked like an old friendship bracelet made out of thread, and some lip balm. Cindy stared oddly at the contents of his hands for a moment before moving on.

"Zack." Mark called out.

"This is going to take a while," Zack said with wry humor.

First he pulled his wallet and a pair of gloves out of his jeans followed by a small knife similar to the one Jeremiah had and followed that up with a travel sized tube of aspirin. Then he pulled a pocket watch, a pack of gum, a small pen flashlight, a compass, and some sugar cubes from his vest pockets.

The man came prepared, Jeremiah could respect that. As soon as he had begun stuffing everything back in his pockets Mark called out Hank's name.

Jeremiah turned eager eyes on the big man. As it turned out he was only carrying lens cleaner for the cameras and some cloths. Jeremiah wasn't sure what he'd expected. If Hank had been carrying something incriminating Jeremiah had no doubt the other man would have been clever enough to hide it before Cindy and Traci reached his side.

"Okay, Norman, you're up," Mark called.

The cinematographer pulled a pair of earplugs, sunglasses, a handkerchief and a folded up piece of paper out of his pockets. Cindy touched the piece of paper and he flinched. "That's private."

"Then she's definitely going to need to take a look at it," Mark said gruffly.

Cindy picked up the piece of paper, carefully unfolded it and began to read it silently. Her cheeks flushed after a couple of seconds and she folded it back up and returned it. "It's a love letter," she said.

"Okay. Let's move on to Wayne."

Cindy and Traci moved over to him. Jeremiah remembered that Wayne was the one who had taken a swing at Kyle on another job. He wondered what they would find in Wayne's pockets.

"Supposin' I don't want to play?" Wayne asked.

The guy was big and strong looking. He wasn't as tall as Hank, but he would still be formidable in a fight.

"Then I'll just have to make you play," Mark said, his voice taking on more of an edge.

"You and what army?" Wayne asked, squaring off his stance and clearly preparing himself for a fight.

"Don't need an army when you've got a rabbi," Mark said.

Jeremiah shook his head, wishing Mark hadn't said that. He dutifully walked over, though, and planted himself in front of Wayne. The other man was definitely getting ready for a fight. In fact, it seemed like he was almost spoiling for one. That wasn't good on any level. Jeremiah had no doubt about his own ability to put the man down, but it would require him to expose more of himself to the others present than he wanted to.

He waved his hand down by his side and he could see the others moving back out of the corners of his eyes. Then he stepped right up to Wayne, invading the man's personal space. From the widening of his eyes he could tell that Wayne wasn't used to someone being that bold.

Jeremiah allowed his face to change so that it hardened. No one else could see it but Wayne. For only the second time since starting his new life he let his old one shine through. "How many men have you killed?" he asked so softly that no one else could hear.

Wayne blinked, clearly surprised by the question. "Shot a couple while in the army," he said gruffly.

Jeremiah shook his head almost imperceptibly. "How many have you killed with your bare hands?"

"None," Wayne said, his voice dropping to a whisper.

"Then you should take a step back right now."

The man took half a dozen steps back, his hand diving into his pocket. "This is all I'm carrying, I swear it," he said. He lifted his money clip high for everyone to see. It was completely stuffed with cash. The exterior bill was a hundred dollar one and Jeremiah was willing to bet the rest were as well.

His actions made perfect sense now. The only question was why had he wanted the money clip to stay hidden? Was it because he was afraid the money would somehow incriminate him or because he didn't trust someone there not to steal it?

Mark whistled low. "Any particular reason you needed all that money on a cattle drive?"

Wayne dropped his eyes. "My ex-wife has to pay me alimony. She likes to pay in cash and I didn't have a chance to get to the bank. Didn't want to leave it in the house."

His son was staring at him in confusion. "Mom pays you alimony? Seriously?"

Wayne turned red, but didn't say anything.

"Okay, moving on," Mark said. "Junior, your turn to show the ladies what you've got."

Junior turned away from his father in time to leer at both Cindy and Traci. "Oh, I'll be more than happy to show them what I've got."

Wayne glanced at Jeremiah quickly. "Shut up, Junior."

"Why should I?"

"Because I'll take it out of your hide if you don't," Wayne said ferociously.

Junior hunched his shoulders but pulled an iPod and some gum out of his pockets.

Wayne glanced again at Jeremiah who nodded and stepped back. Clearly he had put the fear of G-d into the man. Hopefully he'd keep his son in line for the duration of the trip.

"Okay, Liz, you're up," Mark said.

"Way ahead of you," Liz said. She was holding up some paper, a pen, safety pins, a packet of moist towelettes, a comb, lip gloss, a small makeup brush, and a compact with loose powder.

Cindy and Traci inspected everything and then nodded to Mark.

"Okay, Tex, you're up last," Mark said gruffly.

Tex pulled gloves and a tin of chewing tobacco out of his pockets without a word and handed them over to Cindy and Traci who quickly returned them.

"Okay, that's it," Cindy said, turning to Mark.

"Someone should go out and check Curly," Traci said.

"And Roddy, wherever he is," Cindy chimed in.

"Curly couldn't have gotten to the salt to grab it after Brent used it because he was still out there with the cattle and horses," Jeremiah said. "Same is actually true for Tex and Zack."

"So, no need to check any of their gear," Mark said. "We do, however, need to check everyone else's."

"Over my dead body," Junior huffed.

"Don't push me right now," Mark said, "because I'm sure that could be arranged."

"He won't give you any trouble," Wayne said quickly with another glance at Jeremiah.

Junior glanced at his father in surprise. There was enough respect and fear in his eyes, though, that Jeremiah knew they didn't have to worry.

"Before we start searching luggage, we should find Roddy," Jeremiah suggested. He didn't like that the man was still gone. If he was Kyle's would-be killer he'd had plenty of time to destroy any evidence. Of course, he wasn't eager to have his own bags searched and it would make things so much easier if Roddy was the killer.

Mark nodded. "Jeremiah, you and Zack go look for Roddy. Make sure you stick together."

Jeremiah nodded. It was clear that Mark still didn't completely trust Zack. He made eye contact with the cowboy and together they begin to head out toward the horses.

Behind him he could hear Mark saying, "Okay, we're all going to just sit tight and wait for them to get back. So, everyone better get comfy."

"So, what exactly did you say to that guy Wayne to get him to back down like that?" Zack asked.

Jeremiah shrugged. "I just told him that he was making himself look guilty and that he wouldn't want to see what Mark would do to him if he thought he was the killer."

"Smart. I would have thought he could come to that conclusion on his own, though."

"You know, people sometimes don't think clearly when it comes to money and he was clearly trying to hide his."

"I wonder what Roddy's trying to hide," Zack mused.

"He's been gone long enough that I was frankly thinking the same thing."

"We should grab a couple of horses. It will make the search go faster."

"Faster is definitely better."

Zack eyed him speculatively. "I've seen you ride. You're pretty good. Can you ride bareback?"

"Yes," Jeremiah said reluctantly.

"Good, that will save some time."

In another minute they had reached the horses. They unhobbled a couple of the horses and with only hackamores on them went ahead and mounted up.

Jeremiah's horse was bony and not the most comfortable to sit on bareback, but time was of the essence.

He turned, scanning the horizon, looking for any signs of Roddy. No horses were missing so wherever the man was he couldn't have gotten too far. Jeremiah just wondered why they couldn't see him.

They rode out toward the herd and Curly trotted over to greet them. "You can't be relieving me already?" he asked, with a confused look.

"Sorry. We're actually looking for one of the film crew, Roddy. Apparently he came out to get me and never came back to camp," Zack said.

"I haven't seen him, but he's probably just walking around somewhere. He'll show up I'm sure."

"We haven't got the luxury of waiting for that to happen," Jeremiah said grimly.

"Why's that?"

"Cookie was murdered, poisoned," Zack said.

Curly stared at him in disbelief. "The hell you say?"

"It's true," Jeremiah said. "We're worried that Roddy might have done it and is somewhere destroying evidence."

"Then we better find him," Curly said, voice hardening.

Cindy and Traci sat together and Cindy felt like half of her life was spent waiting as they kept craning their necks to see if Jeremiah and Zack were coming back yet. Mark was, in fact, the only one who hadn't gone ahead and sat down. He stood, surveying them all as though they were a bunch of criminals who would try and escape at any moment. At least he wasn't holding his gun, but his stance was suggestive of an ability to whip it out at any sign of trouble.

She had actually never been so intimidated by him before. She'd heard rumors of what had happened during the whole Green Pastures debacle. She'd heard he had tortured a man. Watching him now she could believe it.

The way he kept glancing at Traci made it clear that he was anxious for her safety. With Mark standing watch over them Cindy found herself feeling much more anxious about Jeremiah's well-being than her own.

While she sat and waited she tried to run down everything she knew about those present. She hoped it was Roddy. That would make life simple. By his prolonged absence he certainly looked guilty. She wasn't sure, though. There was something nagging at the back of her mind, some detail she felt like she was not giving the weight it deserved.

There weren't that many suspects, that many people that could have done it. She wasn't sure if that made things better or worse. The truth was whoever had killed Brent had been sleeping within a few feet of her the last couple of nights and that gave her chills. She couldn't go through another night with a killer in their midst.

She looked over at Kyle. He was sitting by himself, whether by his choice or by everyone else wanting to steer clear of him she didn't know. He looked dazed and even a bit scared. She realized that her brother, the crazy adventurer, was at last completely outside of his comfort zone.

And instead of it making her happy, it made her really sad. She had always hated the way he took unnecessary risks and had always wished he would have a healthier respect for danger and learn to steer clear of it. She'd never wanted him to be afraid like she was, though. Nobody should have to live with the kind of fears she'd been carrying around since they were kids.

Her heart went out to him. She touched Traci's arm. "I'm going to go talk to Kyle," she said softly.

"No hitting this time," Traci said, forcing a smile.

"No hitting," Cindy agreed.

She got up slowly. Mark's head swiveled toward her and she fought the sudden urge to put her hands in the air. Instead she turned and walked slowly over to Kyle. As she did she felt like everyone's eyes were on her, not just Mark's. It made her feel like she had a giant target painted on her back and she didn't like that.

Finally she sat down on the ground next to Kyle.

"How are you doing?" she asked.

"How do you think?"

"I can only base that on how I felt the first time I knew somebody was trying to kill me," she said. "It was terrible. On a very deep level, though, it just reinforced my views about how dangerous the world is. For you, I can't imagine."

"I feel so out of control and I don't know how to handle it."

"You're out of control all the time with your job, the stunts you do, the risks you take, all of it."

He shook his head. "It's different. All of those things are very carefully planned, safety checked and double checked. Then, what risk there is in the end, is mine. I take it. I choose it. This...this I didn't choose."

Her brother was a control freak. It surprised her, although watching how he had tried to coordinate everything that had been happening the last couple of days she realized it shouldn't have. He didn't have a director because he had to be the one controlling every detail of what happened.

She squeezed his hand. "I'm sorry this is happening to you."

"I can't believe you've lived through this. More than once. How do you do it?" he asked.

"I have good friends who help me through, and I rely on God a lot, and the rest of the time I just freak out until it's over."

She said the last hoping to get him to smile. It didn't work. Instead he looked at her. "It's more than that. You take charge. You solve the crime. You bring the killer to justice."

"I survive."

"No, you *thrive*," he said.

She blinked, startled at the thought.

"I've been watching you. You're a different person than the last time I saw you. At first I thought it had something to do with Jeremiah, but I'm starting to realize it's more than that. It's you. You've changed, grown. You take control of situations instead of letting them control you."

"I don't think I've grown that much yet," she said with a raised eyebrow.

"You don't think so because the change is too gradual for you to really see. Trust me, though, it's almost like you're a completely different person. The old Cindy would never have hit me."

"That was the PTSD," she hastened to say.

"No, that was you. That was you being bold and taking action. Maybe it wasn't the right choice, at least, that's how my eye feels, but it was a choice. It was something the old you would never have done."

"Still, I'm sorry I hit you," she said.

"No, you're not. Neither am I. I like this Cindy, I feel like I can talk to you."

"You can talk to me," Cindy said. "I'm here to help. And don't worry, we will catch this killer."

Kyle shuddered. "I just can't believe someone would want to hurt me. I mean, other than you."

She bit her lip to keep from laughing at that.

Wrong. Inappropriate. Don't laugh.

But she wanted to so badly.

"Look on the bright side. At least it happened on this trip while I'm here to help you out."

"And I was just thinking 'Why this trip?' I wish it was a different one. I just wanted you guys to have some fun."

Why this trip?

The question rattled around in her mind. It was an excellent question. Honestly, of all the shows Kyle did this particular episode of this particular show had to be the most safe thing he'd done in years, at least on the surface of it. It was safe enough he'd felt like he could bring along his danger-adverse sister. On this trip it would be so much harder to make things look like an accident.

That hadn't stopped someone from trying, though. The frayed saddle strap could have easily passed as an accident. It was odd, though, because while the odds of him falling off his horse because of it were incredibly high it didn't follow that the fall would kill him. Death by food poisoning would seem like an accident, but given how fast it had killed Brent, it would have still been very suspicious and an autopsy would have revealed the true cause of death. A fall while ziplining or smashing his head against a rock while doing intense white water rafting would be much more likely to fly under the radar of suspicion.

So, why hadn't the killer tried before? What had changed? And why couldn't they wait until they filmed one of the next couple of episodes where things could very well be more dangerous to make their move?

Her mind returned to the three cowboys. They were the only ones who wouldn't have any other real opportunity to take down Kyle. What grudge could one of them be holding, though? Kyle didn't even know any of them.

Or maybe the real reason was that someone hadn't thought this through as well as they should have. Maybe they just snapped. The missing Roddy could easily fit that bill. But why not quit instead of commit murder?

She shook her head. The poison. That was something that couldn't have been done spur of the moment. Someone had to plan ahead for that. It had to be someone in the group, too, since the truffle salt had to have been poisoned after the first night's dinner.

"Penny for your thoughts?" Kyle said, breaking the silence.

She turned to him and smiled. "Just trying to figure it all out."

"Maybe I can help."

"That would be good. You can certainly help me fill in some of the gaps, maybe help me figure out a motive."

"Beyond the whole someone clearly hates me thing?"

She was about to explain to him what she'd been thinking about in regards to the timing when a shout brought her up short.

She turned and saw two horses riding toward them at breakneck speed.

11

Mark tensed as Jeremiah and Zack reigned up in front of them. Jeremiah slid off his horse, without any sign of difficulty. He had been riding bareback.

"What is it?" Mark asked.

Jeremiah tossed him a torn beige jacket that had blood on it. Mark wrinkled his nose as he held the thing.

"That's Roddy's jacket," Kyle said, starting up from his seat on the ground.

"That's all we found of him," Jeremiah said grimly.

"You think he was murdered?" Mark asked. If that was true it had to have been one of the cowboys. They were the only ones not with the rest of the group when Roddy was sent to find Zack.

"Or, he wants us to think so," Jeremiah said.

"Well, which is it?" Mark asked impatiently.

"There's no way to tell," Zack said as he, too, slid off his horse. "We found it caught on some brambles. There's enough blood to be clear that's what it is, but not enough to signify that he had a mortal wound of some sort."

"What killer would hide the body and leave the jacket behind?" Cindy asked.

"Where could Roddy have hidden himself?" Traci chimed in.

"None of the horses are missing so he either found someplace he could hole up and not be found or he had a horse waiting for him. If this is him trying to throw us off his scent, that is," Jeremiah said.

"A horse waiting for him? That would indicate an outside accomplice," Mark said. "How would they know where we were going to camp for the night?"

"This is where we always camp on the second night of this particular cattle drive," Zack said.

Mark didn't like it. This whole situation was spinning farther and farther out of control. He forced himself to take a deep breath. "Am I right that the closest town to us at this point is Righteousness?" he asked.

"Yes, that's right," Tex spoke up.

"Okay. We need to send for the Sheriff or whoever is in charge in Righteousness to come out here," Mark said. "This is a crime scene and we need to stay put until they can sort everything out."

He turned and scanned the cowboys. "I think we need to keep the doctor here, just in case."

Tex stepped forward. "I know the way well enough to keep going in the dark with the moon as full as it's going to be tonight. Plus, my horse is faster than Curly's. I can get there by noon tomorrow. I can have the sheriff back here the day after."

Mark pursed his lips. They had to figure forty-eight hours until help arrived. A lot could happen in that amount of time. Still, if that was the best they could do...

"Okay, head out. Leave everything you absolutely don't have to have."

"I'm ready to go now," Tex said.

"Then go."

Tex turned and made his way to grab his gear for his horse.

Jeremiah walked over. "Are you sure it's a good idea to let him go?" he asked.

"I don't see as we have much of a choice," Mark said with a sigh. "We're just going to have to hope for the best."

"And prepare for the worst," the rabbi muttered.

"So what else is new?"

"We should set up watches."

"And just who, besides the four of us, are we going to trust for that?"

"Kyle. He's the intended victim. He can take a turn watching," Jeremiah said.

"Won't hear any argument from me on that one. We shouldn't let him do it alone, though. That will just make him a tempting target."

"Agreed."

"I call not sitting watch with Kyle," Mark said swiftly. It was juvenile, but there was no way he wanted to spend three hours alone with that guy. He just irritated him too much. Looking at Jeremiah's face he wasn't sure, though, that he wanted the other man sitting up with him either.

"Let's get Traci to do it."

Mark rolled his eyes. "She'll love that." Still, it was a much better plan and he couldn't argue with it.

A minute later Tex rode up on his horse. He nodded to Mark and then touched his heels to his horse's flanks and galloped off.

"I hope he gets back with help soon," Mark muttered.

Jeremiah hoped they could identify the killer before local law enforcement showed up. He didn't need any more police asking questions, some of which he was bound to not be able to answer. Having Mark involved in his life was bad enough, but at least they seemed to have a sort of uneasy truce. Mark would ask a question, Jeremiah would refuse to answer, Mark wouldn't push. It had been working for them.

"Cattle are restless," Zack said suddenly.

Mark became aware that there was a lot of noise coming from the direction of the herd. It hadn't been that noisy the night before.

"What's wrong?" he asked.

Zack shook his head. "I don't know, but Curly and I should go see if we can settle them down."

Mark nodded. "Okay."

He had no idea how much of what he'd seen in old westerns about cattle stampedes was true, but he knew he didn't want to find out firsthand. The two cowboys headed for the horses and he turned back to Jeremiah.

"We've got to see if we can find that truffle salt, or anything else incriminating, before it's too late."

"I have a feeling it already is," Jeremiah said.

"You think Roddy took it with him?"

"I don't know, but there's been plenty of time for someone to do something with it."

"All the more reason to finish what we started."

Cindy was on edge. Roddy was missing and now Tex was heading to town. At least, she hoped that's where he was going. It was possible that he was the killer and Mark had just set him free to sneak back in the middle of the night and finish what he'd started. The thought gave her chills.

With Zack and Curly checking on the herd they were that much more fragmented. That made four people that she couldn't keep in sight and that made her more nervous than she cared to admit.

It wasn't enough just to keep an eye on Kyle either. By her count the killer had already tried to get him three times and each time missed and gotten someone different. Two were dead, Martin and Brent. She had been lucky to survive her encounter with just a sprained ankle. The killer was so lousy at getting their target that all of them were in danger.

The fact that there had been three attempts on Kyle's life and three misses had led her to stop and ponder whether he really was the target or whether this was about the production itself. Her gut told her, though, that it was about Kyle. The killer couldn't have known that the truffle salt would have been consumed by anyone else or that Kyle would switch horses with her at the last second. Only Martin's death was even possibly unconnected to Kyle in her mind, but even that she doubted.

"Okay, here's what we're going to do," Mark said, addressing the group. "Cindy and Traci are going to search everyone's gear as planned just in case someone managed to hide that truffle salt."

"Why them?" Norman asked, looking nervous.

"Because they're the only two here I trust," Mark said. "As far as I'm concerned anyone else could be behind this."

Cindy glanced quickly at Jeremiah, hoping he wasn't thinking Mark actually suspected him. His face was calm, though, betraying very little emotion at all. Next she glanced at her brother who looked a little irritated.

"Well, I think it's safe to say I'm not behind this," Kyle said.

Mark shrugged. "For all I know you are. You could be trying to make it look like someone is after you."

"Why on earth would I do that?" Kyle asked, eyes widening.

"Half a dozen reasons that I alone can think of," Mark said. "I'm sure there are more."

Cindy sympathized. Back when they had first met she had been on the other side of Mark's suspicions and it wasn't a pleasant place to be.

"Okay, after they finish going through everything, we're all going to try and just relax," Mark said.

Cindy fought the urge to roll her eyes. That would be a lot easier said than done.

"Then we're going to get some rest. We're going to have guards posted to make sure nothing happens while the rest of us are asleep. Traci and Kyle will take the first watch. Jeremiah and Cindy will take the second. I'll take the third. Any questions?"

Cindy glanced around and noticed that everyone was studiously looking at the ground. If there were any objections, they weren't forthcoming. Of everyone, only Traci looked pleased. Cindy felt herself smiling. Even despite everything it was nice to know that Traci could enjoy the time spent with one of her favorite celebrities. Cindy didn't understand it, but she was happy that Traci was making the most of a bad situation.

"Okay, Traci, you and Cindy get started going through people's gear. And don't be shy about it."

Cindy blushed, not relishing the thought of pawing through people's private things, but she knew there was no other choice.

"We'll start with the stuff that's still close to the wagon. It would have been easy for someone to stash something there," Traci said.

Cindy nodded. The logic was sound and the two of them moved that direction.

"I want to go back out and check again for Roddy," she heard Jeremiah say.

"I'll go with him," Hank volunteered.

"Okay," Mark said after a moment's hesitation.

Cindy didn't like it. That was more people that she couldn't keep tabs on. She also didn't like Jeremiah being alone with Hank. She said a silent prayer for his safety even as she knelt down on the ground next to what she thought was Tex's bag.

"Ready?" Traci asked her as she picked up another bag.

"No."

"Me either. Just keep telling yourself that cops have to rummage through people's things all the time."

That thought might make this all easier on Traci but it didn't make Cindy feel any better. If anything it reinforced her desire to not be a cop. Grimacing, she unzipped the bag and looked inside.

Jeremiah hoped that neither Cindy nor Traci would find the survival knife he had wrapped in a T-shirt and buried in the bottom of his bag. If they did, it could be explained, he just hoped he didn't have to.

Far more worrisome to him was Hank volunteering to help him search for Roddy. He had hoped to be on his own, free to follow his own instincts regarding where Roddy had gone and what had happened to him. Now, he'd have to be careful what he did and watch his back at the same time.

Together they walked a few yards away from the camp. Jeremiah stopped and Hank turned to look at him.

"When Kyle sent Roddy to get Zack, which way did he run, did you see?" Jeremiah asked.

He had only seen Roddy head out in this general direction out of the corner of his eye as he had been working on Brent.

"I only saw him run a little ways, but it was toward the herd, where he would have thought Zack was."

"But we know that Zack didn't see him on his way in. So, in theory, somewhere between here and there is when he turned aside either by his own will or someone else's."

"It makes sense," Hank said, his face a mask.

"He didn't take one of the horses, so unless he had a horse waiting for him somewhere, he would have been on foot. Either way, we have a better shot I think at figuring out which way he went if we stay on foot, too. We'll see what he saw and hopefully something will stick out."

They walked slowly, eyes sweeping back and forth. There were tracks in the dirt but too many people had been crossing back and forth for Jeremiah to tell with any real certainty which ones might be Roddy's. So, instead he looked for disturbed ground to either side that would indicate that Roddy stopped moving toward the herd. He also looked for places where a man could hide himself or even a horse.

The entire time he was painfully aware of the big man walking beside him. Jeremiah kept all his muscles coiled in case he had to move quickly. Why had Hank volunteered to help him? Did he really want to find Roddy or did he want to make sure noone did? Did he mistrust Jeremiah and think him the killer? Or did he plan on making Jeremiah the next to disappear?

After they had gone about an eighth of a mile Hank spoke. "Wayne doesn't scare easily."

Jeremiah refused to give any sign that he knew what the other was referring to. "Is that a fact?"

"It is."

They walked several more feet in silence.

"What did you say to him?" Hank asked.

"Not much. I just reminded him that he was a suspect in a murder investigation and he should cooperate with the police."

That was two people now who were questioning how he had gotten Wayne to play nice. That wasn't good. It was better than if he had to fight the man, though. Then everyone would be questioning him.

"I don't believe you."

Jeremiah stopped and turned to Hank, surprised that the other man was being so honest in his opinion at that moment.

"Really, why not?" Jeremiah asked, carefully modulating his tone to show mild surprise and curiosity.

"Because I've been watching you. You are not what you seem to be."

Jeremiah forced a smile onto his face. "Really? And what do you think I am?"

"I think you're a man who is considering right now whether or not to kill me."

"If that's what you truly think then why are you not afraid?" Jeremiah countered.

"Because I also think you're a man who has no desire to draw attention to yourself, and you have friends here. Your friends would question what would happen, a little too much, I'm guessing. That would be bad for everyone."

"Some questions should never be asked," Jeremiah said.

"Because they can never be answered," Hank countered.

"I think that you're hiding something."

"You know that I am," Hank said.

"I don't know what yet, or for what purpose."

"I have a feeling you will before this journey is done."

"That's supposing that both of us are still alive."

"Supposing," Hank acknowledged.

Jeremiah locked eyes with the man. He was used to seeing fear in men's eyes when they understood even the smallest part of his true nature. In Hank's he saw no fear, only grudging respect.

"I will not hesitate," Jeremiah said, acknowledging that he would kill him if need be.

"Nor will I."

"We have an understanding then." It was a statement, not a question.

Hank nodded anyway.

"Good. Now let's see if we can't find Roddy or whatever's left of him."

"I also believe he's dead," Hank said.

Jeremiah couldn't help but wonder if Hank believed that because Hank had actually done the deed himself. The problem was, while he had been working on Brent, he had been only vaguely aware of those gathered around and he could not have said who was and was not there or who was there who might have left. He grit his teeth and turned back to the search at hand.

"I don't think you need to search Jeremiah's bag," Traci said quietly.

Cindy looked up at her. "But Mark said everyone's." She had Jeremiah's bag in her hands. She had been holding it for almost a minute, uneasy about opening it. It was an invasion of his privacy.

"And we both know that none of the four of us did this," Traci said. "I have no intention of searching your bag or Mark's. You can search mine if you really want to."

"No, that's okay, I guess."

"Look, I get it. It's bad enough that we have to go through strangers' stuff, but you know Jeremiah, you're friends with him. And, clearly, you're not yet ready to have that age-old question answered."

"What question is that?" Cindy asked.

Traci smirked. "Boxers or briefs."

Cindy felt herself flush to her roots.

"Aha! I knew that was what had you worried," Traci said triumphantly.

"Worried, might be a tad strong," Cindy said, struggling to regain what was left of her dignity.

"Oh, come on, I've been sitting here watching you stare at that bag and I could see the curiosity but it just wasn't strong enough to override your shyness."

"Sense of decency, you mean," Cindy practically snapped.

"It's not like you were going to be staring at him in his underwear, just his underwear."

"I don't want to talk about this," Cindy said, dropping the bag when she realized she was still holding it.

"Okay," Traci said. "But we're finished up here, so if you did want to discuss, now would be the time."

"Nothing to discuss."

Traci rolled her eyes. "You know sooner or later you have to talk to somebody about how you feel. It might as well be me now."

"We are in the middle of a murder investigation," Cindy protested, trying to get the other woman back on track.

"When aren't we? Or you at least?"

"I-I don't know. All the time."

"Never. Look, if you're not ready to talk about how you feel about Jeremiah that's okay. I just think you should talk to someone soon before things get more complicated."

Cindy felt a headache coming on. "Let's just get back to the others so we can break the bad news about not finding anything."

"Okay," Traci said, with an exaggerated sigh.

They stood up and walked back to where Mark and the others were closer to the wagon. As they approached Mark raised an eyebrow and they both shook their heads.

"No luck," Traci said.

Mark looked frustrated. "Thanks for trying, ladies."

"What do we do now?" Liz asked.

"Now, we wait for reinforcements," Mark said.

Jeremiah and Hank rejoined the group and Cindy was relieved to see that Jeremiah was okay. Neither he nor Hank looked happy though.

"We couldn't find any trace of Roddy," Jeremiah said.

"The news just keeps getting better and better," Mark said with a sigh.

"Nothing left to do but wait," Hank said.

"Okay, let's build a fire," Mark said. "Cindy, Traci, can you see if there's any food that we can guarantee hasn't been tampered with that we can use for the next couple of days? Not everyone finished dinner and I'm not sure we should at this point."

"I'm pretty hungry," Kyle said quietly.

Cindy had forgotten that unlike many of them Kyle and she hadn't had a bite to eat. Neither had Zack or Curly. Her stomach rumbled noisily. "I'm sure we can find something," she said, pulling Traci toward the wagon.

A couple of hours later things almost seemed normal. Traci and Cindy had found enough canned food to ensure that they all wouldn't starve and had made sure that those who hadn't eaten had before offering up the rest of the food they had heated up to those who had already at least had something.

They had more than enough to supply them until the sheriff arrived which was good news for everyone. Fortunately clean up only took a few minutes and then they were free. Traci immediately excused herself to go see how Mark was faring.

Zack and Curly were back out checking on the cattle which still seemed restless and everyone else was settling in around the campfire. It was hard to believe that the whole place was a crime scene. She and Traci had done what they could to disturb as little as they could in the wagon, but sacrifices had needed to be made in order to make sure they could all still eat.

The adrenalin left her body as she walked up to the campfire and Cindy decided it was a good time to take a bathroom break before she collapsed completely. She thought about asking Traci to go with her, but then decided against it. The killer was after Kyle, not her, and besides, everyone else was accounted for. She grabbed her toiletries bag and headed off, moving as swiftly as she could over the uneven terrain.

She made it to the designated bathroom area and went ahead and dry brushed her teeth and got ready for bed while she was there. Finished, she headed back toward the campsite. She had nearly made it back when she heard voices. She slowed, curious.

"I want to shoot him."

Cindy froze as she heard the male voice whisper.

"You can't do that," a second male voice said, speaking low.

She crept closer, heart pounding, as she tried to figure out who the two men were.

"Why not?"

"We'll end up in a world of trouble."

"Not if we're careful, get him away from the others first."

The speakers were just on the other side of a large rock. She pressed against it, trying to lean around to see who was talking. The rational part of her was screaming for her to go get Mark and Jeremiah, but she was afraid that whoever was plotting against her brother would have moved by then and they'd have lost the chance to confront them. She moved closer, but realized there was no way she could see them without being seen herself.

"Look, I know what he did to you, but you just can't kill him."

"Yeah, and who's going to stop me?"

"I will stop you," Cindy declared, stepping around the rock.

12

Cindy's terror was great as she stared down Zack and Curly. They both looked at her in surprise.

Finally Zack said, "Why do you care about a steer?"

Cindy blinked and then asked, "A steer? You're talking about one of the animals?"

"Yes, a particularly nasty one that's dang near already stampeded the herd twice and almost gored Curly and his horse this afternoon. It was one of the fanciest bits of riding I've ever seen that saved them."

"That and the fact that Tex managed to get a rope on the...beast...at the last second," Curly said.

"So, you're talking about killing the steer," Cindy said, relief slowly replacing her terror.

"Yeah, problem is, gunshots can sometimes spook a herd and this one is already acting mighty twitchy," Curly said.

"Plus, we show up minus a steer and it comes out of our pay," Zack added. "Course, we could use the fresh meat now that we're on rations," he added.

She wanted to laugh at the absurdity of it all. They were trying to decide whether or not to turn a vicious animal into hamburger before it hurt someone and she had thought they were plotting the death of her brother.

"I'm...sorry," she said at last, not sure what else to say.

They were both staring at her as though she had grown a second head.

"You know, whatever you guys decide to do with the steer, I'm sure will be the right decision," she said.

"Hold on, did you think we were talking about a person?" Zack asked, light dawning in his eyes.

She bit her lip, not wanting to admit the truth. Finally she nodded.

"And you jumped out here to confront two armed guys by yourself?" Zack asked.

She nodded again.

He whistled low. "That Jeremiah sure is a lucky fellow."

"Wh-why would you say that?" she stammered.

He stared at her for a moment and then shook his head. "My mistake. I thought the two of you..."

"We're not," she said, wondering why everyone kept bringing that up and struggling not to blush *again*. It was getting old.

"His loss," Zack said with a grin.

She had no response to that. She stood, staring at him for a moment, and then managed to get out a strangled, "Night!" before turning and fleeing to the campfire.

She was breathless when she reached it and Jeremiah looked up at her. "What's wrong?" he asked.

She couldn't even begin to figure out how to answer that one. So instead she said, "Nothing, I'm fine. It was just a longer walk than I thought."

She sat down, bumping against him as she did so which just made her thoughts jumble all the more.

"Are you sure you're okay?" he asked, leaning slightly toward her.

"I'm fine," she said, finding it suddenly hard to think. She turned and found Traci staring at her questioningly. "I'm fine," she reiterated for her sake.

"Now that we've established that," Mark said with a roll of his eyes, "I think it's time to think about settling down for the night. It's been a long day and for some of us it's going to be an even longer night."

Cindy couldn't agree more.

They were leaving the fire going since someone would be up and they had built it fairly close to the sleeping area. She could feel slight warmth from the fire as she got into her sleeping bag.

She and Jeremiah had the second watch. She just hoped she could get some sleep before then. With the way her mind was beginning to race, though, it wasn't looking good.

Jeremiah got into the sleeping bag next to hers and she deliberately rolled over, turning her back to him. She squeezed her eyes shut and prayed, trying to bring order to the chaos that was raging inside her.

It was twenty minutes or more before everyone had finished getting ready for bed and actually settled in. She listened as one by one people began to snore, some softly, others much more loudly, until she wondered if every single person there was in a competition.

Jeremiah woke. He heard a soft footstep nearby. He lay still for a moment, taking in his surroundings. He relaxed after a moment. It was probably Traci come to wake him for his shift.

When Traci touched his shoulder he sat up, grateful that he had been prepared for the contact. He hadn't been very deeply asleep, part of his mind still attuned to what was happening around him.

Traci touched Cindy next, startling her awake. Cindy sat up slowly, wide eyes blinking hard. Tomorrow night he'd tell Traci to let Cindy sleep. It was too late for tonight, though.

He got up and walked over toward the fire. He sat down with his back to it so he could observe all those sleeping. As Kyle and Traci settled down in their sleeping bags that left only Zack's empty. He had drawn the first watch for the cattle and wasn't due to be spelled by Curly for a while yet.

Cindy got up slowly, stretching, and he again regretted that they hadn't let her sleep. She had to be exhausted with everything that was happening and her own injury even though it seemed to be greatly improved.

She came over and sat down next to him, yawning, and crossed her arms over her chest, probably trying to get warm. The night air was chilly but the fire at her back should soon have her comfortable. At least, that's what he told himself as he had to stop himself from putting an arm around her to try and help her warm up.

They sat for quite a while in silence. The sounds of the night were all around them and Jeremiah listened carefully, knowing that Zack, Tex and Roddy were all out there somewhere made him uneasy. Zack was supposed to be watching the cattle and that gave him a freedom of movement Jeremiah didn't have at the moment. Tex should be halfway to town, but that didn't mean that was where he was. He might have easily circled back and even now be laying in wait. As for Roddy that was the biggest worry of all. He honestly had no idea what had happened to the man and that troubled him deeply.

"What do you think happened to Roddy?" Cindy whispered quietly.

He smiled. He shouldn't have been surprised that they were both thinking about the same things. They were just far enough away from the others, and the snoring from some of them was loud enough that they should be able to talk freely as long as they were quiet.

"I wish I knew. I didn't find anywhere he could be hiding, that doesn't mean there wasn't someplace out there. With all the tracks it was impossible to follow him and see if there was really a horse waiting for him somewhere."

"Or someone could have killed him and hid the body."

"I keep thinking that's the most likely scenario. The question is why. If Kyle is really the target I can see how everything else was a missed attempt at killing him, but Roddy? Roddy was nowhere near Kyle when he vanished."

"Maybe he saw something?" she suggested.

"Like someone trying to hide or destroy evidence?"

"Yes," she said. "Or maybe he even suspected someone or said the wrong thing to the wrong person."

"Do you know who wasn't with us the entire time we were trying to revive Brent? I was a bit...occupied. I don't know who might or might not have been present."

"I thought only the cowboys were missing, but I could have been wrong," she said. "There was a lot of stress going on."

Jeremiah's chest tightened. "I've been meaning to ask. How are you doing? I know you...liked...Brent."

She turned to look at him and the firelight reflected in her eyes made them smolder.

"Either it hasn't really hit me yet or I'm becoming desensitized to these things I think. I mean, I'm upset, but

I'm more worried about figuring out who did this before someone else gets hurt."

"Still, I'm sorry."

"Brent was really nice. I was shocked when he asked me out, and I didn't really know what to say. I mean, I'm sure he was a great guy, but..."

Jeremiah wished he could decipher the way she was looking at him. He felt himself getting pulled in closer. He forced himself to turn away and he hastily added another log to the fire just for something to do while he cleared his thoughts. Being on watch together was more of a mistake than he had previously thought.

Finished he turned back. Cindy was once again staring out over the sea of sleeping bags. "Who do you think is the killer?" she asked after a moment.

"Given that only one person has actually managed to hurt Kyle my money's on you," he teased to try and shift the mood.

She sighed. "That's not funny."

"It is a little bit, you have to admit it."

"Okay, fine, but just a little bit."

"I mean, if you had asked me a couple of days ago I would have said he was in the most danger from Traci hugging him to death, but she's been a model of restraint."

Cindy smirked. "Wait, it's early yet."

Someone coughed and they both fell silent. There was a rustling and then someone sat up. After a moment Jeremiah recognized it as Norman. The man slowly got up and then headed stiffly in the direction of the restroom area. He was quickly swallowed up by darkness. Jeremiah briefly contemplated following him, but that would mean leaving Cindy alone and he wasn't about to do that.

Beside him he could feel her tension. Clearly she wasn't happy with having him wander off either.

"That note you found in his pocket, you said it was a love letter."

"Yes," she said, sounding intensely uncomfortable.

"Was it to him or from him?"

"To him. It started 'My dearest Norman'."

"Did you see who wrote it?"

"No, I assumed it was a girlfriend. I didn't read very far. It was pretty personal."

"Do you think it could have been from Liz?"

"I never thought about it, why?" she asked, startled.

"Generally speaking guys aren't in the habit of carrying around love letters in their pockets. With cell phones they rarely even carry around pictures anymore."

"So, you think it's something he got since arriving and not before?"

"It's just a theory."

"Liz and he don't act like a couple," Cindy said.

"Maybe they're hiding it for a reason. Or maybe Liz didn't write it."

They fell silent as a figure approached out of the dark. It was Norman returning. A minute later he was back in his sleeping bag.

They sat in silence a while longer before Cindy asked, "Did you ever carry around a picture of a girl in your wallet?"

"Yes," he answered.

"Oh, who?" she asked, her voice sounding a bit odd.

Jeremiah smiled. "Her name was Alize, it means Joyful and noone ever lived up to a name more than she did. She was beautiful, long golden, red hair. We used to spend every moment of every day together. I miss her terribly."

"I'm sorry," Cindy said. "What happened to her?"

"She died."

"Oh, that's terrible!"

"It took me a long time to get over it. I never thought I'd have another dog again, but then Captain came into my life and changed all that."

"Dog? Alize was a dog?" she asked, sounding strangled.

"Yes, beautiful Golden Retriever that I had as a kid. She made it to fourteen, which was a good, long life. How about you?"

"No, no dogs."

"No, I mean, ever carry a picture of a boy around in your purse?"

"I went to Homecoming my sophomore year of high school with Michael Fowler. Wc had our picture taken and I carried that picture in my purse for quite a while. His family moved away shortly after that, though."

"So, you never heard from Michael again?" he asked.

"We wrote a few times, but you know how it is."

He wasn't sure he did. He was sure, though, that the way he was feeling at the moment it was a very good thing that Michael Fowler was nowhere to be found.

Cindy couldn't believe the wave of emotions that had been filling her for the last few minutes. Sorrow, curiosity, relief, and most startlingly, deep, intense jealousy. She had been nearly overcome with it when she thought Alize was a girl. She and Jeremiah had never really had a conversation about past boyfriends and girlfriends and she found that she really, really didn't want to know because the thought of him being with someone else upset her.

Not that she had any right to be upset. They weren't together, he wasn't hers. She couldn't help but think, though, about what Traci had said about her needing to discuss her feelings about Jeremiah with someone soon.

She was beginning to think she was right. Besides, if things continued this way she might find herself accidentally discussing those feelings with Jeremiah before she was even willing to admit them to herself.

Is it the shared danger that brings us together? she couldn't help but wonder. *Or is it something more than that?*

She closed her eyes for a moment. Kyle had told her that she had changed a lot. Maybe that was true. Some days she felt it more than others. How much of that was because of Jeremiah, his friendship and the things that he brought out in her?

She opened her eyes. The middle of the wilderness surrounded by cattle and potential killers was not the place to have such deep thoughts. She needed to focus on the task at hand which was getting everyone home alive.

One of the sleepers stirred and began to sit up. At the same time she heard something walking toward them from her right.

"It's time for Curly to take over the watch from Zack," Jeremiah whispered.

A moment later she saw Zack walking toward them leading a horse. Curly got up and crossed silently over to him. He took the reins from Zack.

"They're calming down finally. Still more restless than I would like," Zack said softly.

"Wonder what's got them so spooked tonight?" Curly said.

Zack shrugged. He turned and tipped his hat to Cindy and Jeremiah.

Cindy gave a little wave. If they were trading shifts that meant hers and Jeremiah's should be half over. It was actually going by faster than she would have imagined.

The two cowboys were lost in discussion and she couldn't help but wonder what they'd decided to do about the renegade steer that was causing them problems. She wasn't about to ask, though, and then have to explain it all to Jeremiah.

Over in the sleeping area Mark stirred and sat up slowly, rubbing at his eyes. Cindy was about to go over and tell him that he didn't have to get up yet when she stopped.

Jeremiah had cocked his head to the side as though listening intently to a sound that she couldn't hear. Zack and Curly had both stopped talking and also seemed to be listening. Something was wrong, she felt it deep down. A second later she heard the sound of galloping hooves. She turned and looked at Jeremiah uncertainly.

He shook his head. "That's way too fast for Tex to have reached town and sent help."

"Who do you think it could be?" Mark asked, voice strained, looking suddenly very alert.

"I don't know," Jeremiah said, "but something tells me it isn't good."

Others began to stir and sit up as the sound grew louder. Cindy felt like she was holding her breath, waiting to find out what was going on and who the rider could be.

Finally a horse appeared out of the darkness. He was moving fast and heading straight for the campfire.

"He's not slowing up," Jeremiah said, springing to his feet at nearly the same time as Zack leaped forward.

"There's no rider!" Zack shouted a moment later.

The horse came barreling toward them and too late Cindy realized she and the others should get out of the way.

Jeremiah and Zack rushed forward, arms up. The horse started to swerve at the last moment and Jeremiah snatched at its bridle. The horse reared for a moment and then came crashing back to the ground. He stood, sides heaving and head bobbing up and down.

"That's the horse Tex was riding," Curly said, his voice strained as he struggled to calm his own mount who had been agitated by all the activity and was prancing from foot to foot impatiently.

"Whoa there, fellow," Zack said, reaching out a hand to the riderless horse. He patted the animal's neck and then touched his hand to the saddle. He pulled his hand away after a moment and brought it under his nose.

"What is it?" Curly demanded.

"Blood."

13

Mark jumped to his feet as chaos seemed to explode around him. Another dead man was the last thing they needed, especially when that particular victim was supposed to be getting them help.

Zack had pulled a flashlight out of his pocket and was inspecting the horse that had returned. Jeremiah was still holding the horse steady and the animal looked exhausted.

Curly was mounting his horse. “We have to go look for Tex. He could be out there hurt,” he said, urgency tingeing his voice.

Zack shook his head. “I don’t think so,” he said quietly. “Not with this much blood. There’s no way he’s alive.”

Mark clenched his fists and took a deep breath, working to keep it together. He felt a light hand on his arm and knew it had to be Traci. He glanced at her and she looked up at him, eyes enormous, worry written all over her face.

Kyle appeared on his other side. “There’s no way anyone could have mistaken Tex for me,” he said quietly.

“No,” Mark agreed. “But someone didn’t want us sending for help.”

“How is that even possible? We were all together?” Kyle said.

“Not all of us, not every moment,” Mark growled. “Not to mention that Roddy is still missing.”

Zack had been carefully going over the horse’s saddle and now he had moved around to the horse’s hindquarters where he was shining the light on the animal’s right flank.

“What is it?” Jeremiah asked him.

"Tex carried a whip on his saddle along with a rope. The whip is missing, but this horse has a nasty cut back here as though someone whipped him to encourage him to run."

"Tex?" Mark asked.

"No, Tex would never have used that on a horse," Curly said.

"Agreed," Zack said.

"So, what, his killer whipped the horse then?" Mark asked.

"That would be my guess. He probably killed Tex then whipped the horse to send him running. Eventually the animal turned and decided to head back to camp."

"Any way to tell how long ago all this happened?" Mark asked. Finding out how far away could help them eliminate suspects. Only Curly and Zack would have access to the horses to ride after Tex and do this. Or, perhaps Roddy had been laying in wait.

On the other hand, Tex might have been the one waiting for someone and he might have been killed for it.

"I can't tell."

"Do you think he was shot?" Mark asked, cursing the fact that his own gun was still under his pillow.

"Can't tell that either. Out here, though, a gunshot could be heard pretty far away. I certainly didn't hear anything. It's possible he was shot, but just as likely he was stabbed. After all, whoever did this was close enough to take the whip."

"And if it was a gun, and they were that close, they might have managed to use his own gun on him. If it was a knife...I'm not even sure we've seen a knife here," Mark said.

"I think the real question is, who had the opportunity to do this?" Cindy asked.

"It most certainly is. Did you see anything while you were on watch?" Mark asked Traci and Kyle.

Traci shook her head. "No, just a couple of people using the bathroom and coming back."

"Who?" Mark asked.

"Liz was first and then later Jeremiah," Kyle answered.

"Norman was the only one who got up to use the bathroom while we were on watch," Cindy volunteered.

"And, of course, we still don't know what happened to Roddy," Jeremiah added.

"Crossing off suspects should make things easier not harder," Mark growled. "Okay, there's nothing more we can really do until daybreak. I suggest those of us who can get some more sleep do so while they can. Zack, take care of the horse and then get some sleep. Curly, you're up on cattle duty, right?"

"Right," Curly said.

"Okay, everyone else hit the hay."

Reluctantly the others started to return to their sleeping bags. Fear hung heavy in the air, though, and Mark doubted anyone would be sleeping well. He knew he couldn't go back to sleep at this point.

"Cindy, Jeremiah, you can go back to sleep, too. I've got the watch from here."

Cindy nodded and trudged over to her sleeping bag, walking beside Traci.

"I'll stay up with you a while, at least until everyone get's settled," Jeremiah said.

Mark nodded. It was a good idea. Two sets of eyes at this point were definitely better than one. He sat down with his back to the fire as everyone dispersed. Jeremiah sat beside him.

A few minutes later Zack returned and once he was in his sleeping bag everything seemed to get pretty quiet. That was good, because Mark needed serious time to think about what the plan for the morning was.

"You awake?" Cindy whispered as softly as she could to Traci.

Traci rolled over and looked at her. "Yes, what is it?"

"I know the timing couldn't possibly be any more inappropriate, but I wanted to tell you that I think you're right."

"About what?" Traci asked with a yawn.

"About me needing to talk to somebody about Jeremiah and soon.

Traci broke out into a grin. "I knew it. So, you want to talk now?"

"No, I want to try to sleep now. I have a feeling tomorrow is going to be crazy."

"Tomorrow? What would you call today?"

Cindy took a deep breath. "Honestly? I have a feeling today was just the dress rehearsal for crazy."

Traci's eyes widened, but she didn't comment.

"So, let's try talking tomorrow," Cindy said.

Traci nodded. After a minute she closed her eyes and rolled over.

Cindy lay, staring up at the stars overhead. She tried to pray, but her mind kept wondering in all sorts of directions. *The dress rehearsal for crazy*. She wished that wasn't true, but she felt instinctively that things were going to get weirder if not downright worse before this was all over.

She yawned and flipped over on her side. A moment later she was asleep.

It was just before dawn and Jeremiah was the only one awake. Mark had finally fallen asleep while sitting upright, his back to the fire. Exhaustion and stress coupled with the darkness and stillness had finally taken their toll. Jeremiah had helped bring that about by being quiet for the last hour and refusing to engage in idle chatter. It was nearly the end of the shift and soon the others would be waking up. Still he had maybe half an hour before they did or Curly put in an appearance. That was just enough time for him to do what he needed to if he was swift and quiet.

He rose noiselessly from his seat by the fire and walked away without the merest whisper of sound, ears listening for any stirrings from those behind him. In a few seconds the chuck wagon loomed in front of him in the early morning darkness, a hulking structure, it's white canvas only reflecting a tiny bit of light from the campfire.

Inside was all the camera equipment containing the footage from the last couple of days. That footage could never see the light of day. Even as he eased himself up into the wagon, though, he couldn't help but wonder who the original saboteur had been. Odds were good that whoever it was had been caught on camera doing something they shouldn't, possibly engineering one of the "accidents" that had happened.

That mystery, though, needed to take a backseat to making sure that all of the footage was destroyed and the cameras disabled going forward. He slid on a pair of disposable gloves he had found in a stash in the wagon earlier when searching for the truffle salt. As he picked up the main camera he struggled not to curse Kyle's name for getting him into all this. He should have known that any vacation involving the television show host would by necessity involve a camera.

He erased the footage, removed the camera battery and found and took the backup batteries as well. Next he turned to the helmet cameras, going through them swiftly but systematically to make sure nothing was overlooked.

At last he gathered all the batteries up and exited the wagon. He walked almost a quarter of a mile away from everything else before stopping to bury them and the gloves in the ground. Finished he made his way back to camp, chasing the coming of the dawn.

Everyone was still asleep as he slid down back into position near the campfire next to Mark. He took a few deep breaths, forcing the adrenaline from his system. He allowed his heart to calm and he sat and watched the first rays of the sun peek over the horizon.

"Was starting to think morning would never get here," he whispered.

"Hmm, what?" Mark asked, coming awake.

"Dawn's here finally," Jeremiah said.

Mark yawned and looked up. "I guess it is."

"I'm going to go change clothes and get ready if it's okay with you."

"Sure is," Mark said, straightening up more and yawning again.

With any luck the detective would think he'd only been out for a minute or two.

Jeremiah got up and crept quietly over to his sleeping bag. His backpack was just behind his pillow and he opened it as quietly as possible to retrieve what he needed. Cindy didn't even stir awake. He fought the urge to linger for a moment and watch her sleep.

A few minutes later when he came back Mark headed off to get ready for the day as well while Jeremiah set about making some coffee.

When Cindy woke in the morning she was surprised to find that instead of one of the last ones up she was one of the first. Jeremiah was already awake, sitting by the fire drinking what smelled like a cup of coffee and eating a protein bar. He smiled at her and she smiled back, feeling more self-conscious than she had the other mornings about him seeing her before she could dress or brush her hair or teeth. She was sure she looked like a disaster.

He, on the other hand, was already dressed and actually looked rested. That was quite a feat and she couldn't help but wonder how he managed to pull that off. She grabbed her stuff and headed off to clean up and get changed.

When she returned a couple of minutes later others were just beginning to stir. Jeremiah offered her a protein bar and she took it. "Thank you," she said as she unwrapped it and sat down next to him.

"I figure it's safe. I brought it with me," he said.

"Wish I'd thought to do something like that."

"Why would you? You were promised a trip with all meals included."

"Then why did you?" she asked around her first bite.

"Oh, you know, just in case," he said vaguely.

"What do you think's going to happen this morning?" she asked as she took another bite.

He shrugged. "I'm guessing that will be mostly up to Mark. Smartest thing in my opinion would be to abandon the cattle and all of us to ride for town as fast as we can."

She winced, knowing that would mean abandoning the wagon as well. She'd have to get back on a horse. Despite the sage advice of the infamous saying she'd secretly hoped to never have to get back up on the horse again.

It must have shown on her face but Jeremiah reached out and touched her shoulder. "Don't worry. I'll personally check your horse and gear this time before we set out."

"Thanks," she said. "I appreciate that."

He was always looking out for her and she was starting to get spoiled. "Thank you again for saving my life the other day."

He looked intensely uncomfortable. "That was nothing," he muttered.

She shook her head. "I've been thinking about it a lot and I'm still not sure exactly what happened, but I do know that I expected things to be a lot worse. I know you saved me somehow."

He dropped his eyes and he muttered something. She wasn't sure what he'd said, but it sounded like "That's what I do".

"Anyway, I figure when we make it out of this mess, I'm going to owe you something cool. Dinner someplace nice or another theme park visit, something."

He looked up and grinned. "Deal."

The grin made her spine tingle in a good way and she felt herself grinning back.

Over in the sleeping area Traci was finally sitting up, yawning and stretching. She turned and glanced at them.

"Where's my husband?" she asked.

"He was walking around a few minutes ago," Jeremiah said. "He should be back any minute."

Cindy could see the look of worry on Traci's face which helped remind her that none of them were safe until they either found the killer or got back to civilization. She glanced around, not liking the fact that she couldn't see Mark.

Mark can take care of himself, she thought, trying to calm the sudden fear in her own heart. She realized in that moment that if something happened to either Traci or Mark on this trip that she'd never forgive herself or her brother.

Kyle was on his way back from the restroom area, looking more tired than she could ever remember seeing him.

He's definitely not ready for his close-up.

She stood up and stretched, trying to hide her own burgeoning concern as she continued to look around.

Curly was standing with Zack over near the chuck wagon and he looked like he, too, was about to fall over. From what she could tell he and Tex had been friends. A surge of pity swelled her heart for him. The cowboys were likely just innocents caught up in this mess like the four of them were.

Wayne and Junior were both busy digging in their own bags looking for whatever it was they were needing for the morning. She still didn't trust either of them.

A few seconds later Liz and Norman appeared heading back from the direction of the bathroom area. Liz was walking with a bounce in her step that Cindy couldn't help but envy. Then again Liz had probably had the luxury of sleeping through most of the night. Liz stopped at her bed and stuffed her pajamas into her bag. Norman kept walking, heading for the chuck wagon.

That left only Hank and Mark unaccounted for.

Well, and the missing Roddy, she reminded herself.

"Where do you think Mark is?" she asked Jeremiah quietly.

He stood slowly to his feet, his face a mask. "Why, you think something's wrong?" he asked, equally quiet.

"I hope not. I'm just getting...worried."

Apparently Traci was too. The other woman was standing up now. Still wearing her pajamas she cupped her hands around her mouth. "Mark!" she shouted, an edge of panic in her voice.

A moment passed then another.

Cindy was just about to start shouting his name as well when she heard an answer. "Coming!"

She sagged in relief and a few moments later Mark appeared from the direction where the horses were, Hank walking beside him.

Traci ran to him and threw her arms around him and hugged him tight. Cindy could feel the other woman's relief and fear as though it were her own and she glanced at Jeremiah, grateful he had been the first person she'd seen when she woke and that she hadn't had to wonder where he was.

"I'm here," Mark said his voice tired and a little gruff. "Don't worry."

With their arrival everyone seemed to gravitate around the campfire as though by some unspoken command.

"Where's Norman?" Mark asked. "I want to go over some of yesterday's footage with him."

"That's going to be impossible," Norman said, face grim as he walked up to them with a camera in hand.

"What do you mean?" Mark asked.

"It's gone."

"Yesterday's footage? Someone is sabotaging it?" Mark asked.

Norman shook his head, a muscle in his jaw quivering. "It's far worse than that. This time someone stole all the batteries, even the backup ones. I'm assuming they erased the footage while they were at it, but until we can reach civilization and get some new batteries I won't be able to tell."

"Well, then we need to get to town as soon as possible," Liz said.

"She's right," Wayne added. "The way I see it we have to abandon everything and get to town as soon as possible. Maybe the footage is still there and the police can figure out the killer from that. If not, though, we'll still be a lot safer there. Out here we're just sitting ducks."

"It's going to be a dangerous ride with a killer among us," Hank said. "We might not want to risk it."

"We can't very well send someone else to town, look what happened to the last guy," Junior snapped.

"The safest thing to do would be to put our heads together and try to figure out who did this," Cindy said.

"Cindy's right," Traci spoke up. "We need to be able to keep an eye on each other until we can figure this out and that's what we should do. It's a long ride to town and who knows what will happen along the way."

"What do you think?" Cindy asked Jeremiah.

"I think we should make a try for town," he said.

She stared at him in surprise. Somehow that wasn't the answer she'd been expecting.

"Don't you think it's too dangerous to make that trek, especially with a desperate killer in our midst?" she asked.

"I don't think we have much of a choice," he said.

She turned to Mark. "Mark, what do you think?"

"I think we sit tight until we have the killer in custody and then head for town."

"But how are we going to figure out who did it?" Zack asked.

"Oh, I'm certain I already know who the killer is," Mark said.

All eyes swiveled toward him.

"Who?" Cindy asked after a moment, feeling somewhat breathless as she waited for him to point the finger. She was stunned that he hadn't already shared the information. He must have just discovered something or put the pieces together in the last few minutes.

"The only person who had the ability to pull all these things off, one who most of you wouldn't even think twice to question."

"Who is it?" Traci urged, eyes wide.

Mark turned and leveled his gaze across the campfire. "The killer among us is Jeremiah."

14

Cindy was thunderstruck. She couldn't have heard Mark right. The two men stood, eyeing each other across the dying fire in the early morning light with everyone else gathered around. For a moment no one moved, no one spoke. No one even seemed to blink.

It was the most absurd thing she'd ever heard. She couldn't have possibly heard Mark accuse Jeremiah of being the murderer. She turned her head slightly, just enough so that she could see Traci. The other woman was staring at her husband, a look of bewilderment on her face.

"The rabbi?" Norman asked, breaking the silence first.

"I don't believe what I'm hearing," Jeremiah said, his voice low.

Cindy wanted to jump in, say that neither did she, but her throat seemed to seize up and she couldn't get a word out. It was all a mistake. A huge, terrible mistake. That was all there was to it.

"Yes, the rabbi. Of course, he's only been a rabbi for a few years. I think the real question is how much do we know about you, really?" Mark demanded.

Jeremiah clenched his fists. "Enough to know that I'm not the bad guy here."

"I'm not so sure of that. You've been acting twitchy ever since you found out this whole thing was going to be filmed. I wouldn't be surprised to find out that you've been the one sabotaging the cameras."

His camera was never turned on the whole first day, the thought came unbidden to Cindy's mind.

"You're insane."

"Am I?" Mark asked. "I think I'm thinking clearly for the first time in a long time. The evidence has been there, right under my nose. You're the only one here clearly capable of doing these things."

"How do you figure?" Jeremiah asked.

"You had means, opportunity, motive and you're a murderer."

"That's a lie," Jeremiah countered.

No, it isn't, Cindy realized as she pressed a shaking hand over her mouth. She knew he'd killed at least one man, she'd seen it. He'd killed a serial killer to save her. But that was self-defense, he had to do it to save them both. That wasn't murder. She felt her heart begin to pound. She had never shared her suspicions about that with anyone. It had all happened so fast there were times even she doubted what she had seen that night.

"I know you killed the Passion Week serial killer," Mark accused.

Something changed in Jeremiah's face.

"And I don't think you stopped there," Mark continued. "I think there's a long trail of bodies stretching out behind you and that's just in the last couple of years. Heaven only knows what you did before then."

"You don't know what you're saying," Jeremiah growled, his voice taking on an edge.

"Don't I? You never talk about your past, not ever, to anyone. I bet even Cindy doesn't know anything about you."

He had a dog. She wanted to speak up, to defend Jeremiah, to tell Mark about the dog. But even as she fought with the lump in her throat she realized that the bit about the dog was the first thing she'd really learned about his past other than that he was born in Israel and had served his mandatory time in the military.

"And that dead guy who showed up on your lawn last year? We could never tie him in with the other murders. The guy behind all that finally confessed to every other crime but that one. He'd never even heard of the guy. So, who was he? Why did you kill him? Was it because he knew who you really are?"

"Stop talking now," Jeremiah hissed, his face contorting.

"And another thing. You have no web presence. Like zero. No pictures online, and your full name isn't even mentioned on your synagogue's website! You know how much effort it takes to keep that far off the radar? A lot! And the only people who do are those with something to hide," Mark continued. Spittle was flying from his mouth and he was gesturing wildly now, his eyes bugging out of his head.

"I don't do social media, so what?"

"It's more than that! It takes concerted effort, frequent effort to wipe yourself away as though you didn't even exist. You've been hiding something from the day we met and now you were afraid Kyle here with his stupid little show was going to bring your entire house of cards crashing down. And just how long was I asleep this morning? Long enough for you to sabotage all the cameras I bet. You were the only one who could have done it, the only one who would have been alone since we turned them all off yesterday."

Cindy blinked. If Mark had really fallen asleep on guard duty then that was true. The few people who had gotten up in the middle of the night had headed for the bathroom in the opposite direction of the chuck wagon and she was sure no one could have gotten in there and done that much damage without being heard.

"And what about Tex? I don't exactly have a gun," Jeremiah said, his voice dripping sarcasm.

"You didn't need one," Mark said, calming slightly. "Zack said it could easily have been a knife that killed Tex."

Mark turned suddenly to Traci and Cindy. "What exactly did you find when you searched his bag?"

Cindy could feel herself turning red as Traci stammered, "We...we didn't actually check his bag."

"What!" Mark barked, eyes bulging again. "Well, go get it now and let's just have a look at whatever the good rabbi might be hiding."

Jeremiah started forward as if to stop them and Mark pulled his gun. "Don't even think of moving," he said, his voice low and dangerous.

Traci ran over, grabbed Jeremiah's bag, and ran back. All around them everyone else was beginning to stir and mutter.

"Okay, go ahead and dump it all out and let's just see what he has in there," Mark said.

Traci unzipped the backpack, pulled out some clothes and dumped them on the ground. Next she pulled out a first aid kit, some fishing line and hook, matches, a small bit of rope, a compass, heating packs, and more protein bars.

At the last she pulled something out of the very bottom of the bag. It was a rolled up T-shirt, but by the look on Traci's face there had to be more to it than that. Slowly

Traci unrolled the T-shirt. There inside was a massive hunting knife.

Cindy gasped and took an involuntary step backward. It wasn't Jeremiah's, it couldn't be. Why else, though, would he have objected to them searching his bag just now? She felt dizzy, like her whole world was caving in around her.

Circumstantial evidence, that's all it is, she told herself over and over again.

Traci looked stricken. "I never dreamed..." she whispered, breaking off in mid-sentence. "I'm so sorry," she said at last, although who she was apologizing to Cindy couldn't tell.

"And I'm willing to bet that when we get that knife to town they'll be able to find trace evidence of blood on it," Mark said, his voice shaking slightly.

His face was flushed, but whether with anger or triumph she didn't know.

"Are you saying he killed Tex?" Curly asked, his voice quivering with rage.

"Tex. Brent. Martin. All of them. Likely Roddy too. Was this all to keep your secret? Or did you just keep missing Kyle?" Mark asked.

"I have nothing to say to you," Jeremiah hissed.

"You know, I shouldn't have been surprised that you were right there to pull Cindy off that horse when the strap broke. After all, you knew it was going to happen so you were riding close enough to look like the hero when it did. It must have really galled you that she and Kyle changed horses at the last minute."

Jeremiah rattled off a string of unintelligible words under his breath that she assumed were curses. He had the look of a man caught in a trap.

Mark picked up the piece of rope that had come out of Jeremiah's backpack and tossed it to Hank.

"Tie his hands, make it good," he ordered. "Jeremiah Silverman, I'm arresting you for the murders of Martin, Brent, and Tex; for the suspected murder of Roddy; and for the attempted murder of Kyle Preston."

"You're making a big mistake," Jeremiah said, "and you will live to regret it."

The tone in which he said it sent a chill down Cindy's spine.

"You have to be wrong," she turned, pleading with Mark.

He stared her straight in the eyes. "I don't think I am," he said. "I've known there was something off about him from the beginning. And, if you're being honest with yourself, I'm guessing you've known it, too."

He turned back to Hank who was just finishing binding Jeremiah's wrists in front of him. "Put him in the wagon until we can figure out what to do next."

Cindy watched helplessly as Hank hauled Jeremiah over to the wagon and practically threw him inside. She had to fix this. She had to find the right killer.

She glanced over at Curly. The man looked like he was capable of murdering Jeremiah right there. *Revenge for his friend's death*, she realized with a shudder. Wayne also looked like he had murder in his heart and she couldn't help remember how Jeremiah had confronted him over revealing the contents of his pockets.

She glanced around at all the other angry, hostile faces and the sick feeling in the pit of her stomach just got worse. Everyone there had lost a friend or a coworker and they wanted blood. On top of that, they were what felt like a million miles away from civilization. With everyone busy blaming Jeremiah, it would also give the real killer plenty of time to dispose of evidence or even fabricate some. By the time they made it to town Jeremiah would look plenty guilty to everyone.

If someone hasn't killed him by then.

Jeremiah was sitting in the wagon, having been shoved into position by Hank before the big man left. Outside the others were no doubt beginning to mull his fate as well as their own. Mark was smarter and a lot more observant than Jeremiah had given him credit for. That had been a mistake, one that he wouldn't be repeating any time soon. The detective had gotten a lot of things right, too close for comfort certainly.

Jeremiah inspected his bonds. The knots on the rope were solid, but he should be able to work himself free in a couple of minutes, even without the help of any of his tools. His Swiss Army knife was currently underneath his pillow. It was probably only a matter of time before they found that as well.

Outside he could hear voices raised in the distance. No doubt they were trying to decide how to proceed. At this point the only real choice they had was to press on. The question was, would they be abandoning the herd? The truth was, they would know they couldn't trust him on horseback so they could only really travel as fast as the wagon could go. After what had happened to Tex they were unlikely to risk sending someone out alone again, even if they thought they had their killer locked up all safe and secure. That gave him more than enough time to escape.

He heard a light footstep outside and he tensed. The wagon moved ever so slightly and a moment later Cindy appeared, pushing through the canvas and letting it fall back in place behind her. Her face was pale, but her eyes were clear. No sign of tears.

"Are you okay?" she whispered.

He took a deep breath. This was the moment of truth. "I'd be better if you said you brought something to cut me loose with," he said tersely, watching her facial expressions closely.

"I'm sorry, I don't have anything like that," she said.

"Then I'm not doing too well."

"Mark is wrong, I know you can't possibly have done all this," she said.

"I appreciate the vote of confidence, but seriously, I'd appreciate more help getting out of this."

"Wait! I just realized something," she said, her voice strained.

"What?"

"This is the chuck wagon. There have to be knives in here somewhere. I just have to figure out where Brent is...was... storing them. Then I can cut you free."

He blinked, nearly unable to contain his surprise. "You'd do that for me?" he asked.

She turned and looked at him. She was so close, a hair's breadth away. "Of course I would. I believe in you," she said. There was a light shining in her eyes and she had never looked more beautiful to him than in that moment.

"And what do you think is going to happen after you cut me loose?" he asked.

"I think you're going to make a run for it. Get clear of here until I can figure out who the real killer is. It's the safest thing given the circumstances."

She was right about that. He was pretty sure there were at least a couple people outside who wanted him dead.

He took a deep breath. "And what if I am the real killer?" he asked.

She stared at him for a moment that seemed to last forever. Finally she knelt down in front of him so that they were face-to-face. She swallowed hard, but she met his eyes. "Then I'm sure you had your reasons," she whispered at the last.

It was the last thing he had expected her to say and it changed everything. Suddenly the very air around them seemed charged. "Run away with me," he whispered.

She reached out and put a hand on his shoulder. It was trembling. "Why?"

"Because I can protect you from the evils of this world. Really protect you, not the shadow of effort I've put in so far."

She sucked in her breath. "That's not your job."

He wanted to reach out, put his hands on her waist, but the way they were tied he couldn't. Instead he leaned forward so they were closer together. The hand she had on his shoulder slipped around behind his head.

"But I want it to be," he said.

She leaned forward, eyes wide, swaying slightly, and he realized she was going to kiss him. He knew he should stop her. There was so much that she didn't know, but he wanted that kiss more than anything he'd ever wanted in his whole life.

Her lips were an inch from his, her eyes were closed, and he knew in another moment he'd be lost forever.

"Hey, what are you doing in there!" a harsh voice demanded.

Cindy sat back, startled, eyes wide. "Just talking," she managed to say.

It was good that she could answer because he was speechless.

Curly poked his head inside the canvas. "You best get on out of there, Miss," he said, his eyes hard and his face angry.

Cindy stood slowly, a look of dismay on her face.

Jeremiah took a ragged breath, trying to gather his wits about him. From the look on the cowboy's face he could tell the man had some sort of old fashioned western justice on his mind. He might stop short of lynching Jeremiah for killing his friend, but that didn't mean he wouldn't try beating him within an inch of his life.

Cindy must have sensed the same thing because she looked at Curly and said, "Would you come with me to talk to Kyle about canceling the rest of this cattle drive?"

He looked like he was about to argue with her, but apparently thought better of it. "Yes, Miss, that seems like a good idea," he said, casting one last threatening glance at Jeremiah before leaving with her.

Jeremiah listened to the sounds of their retreating footsteps and then leaned his head forward into his bound hands. They were shaking and he fought a silent battle with himself. His actions, his words had been purely selfish. He hadn't had Cindy's best interests at heart when she was kneeling there in front of him.

She had been so agitated that she hadn't been thinking clearly. All the more reason why he should have been thinking for the both of them. The more he was with her, though, the less rational he seemed to become. His thoughts had started straying into forbidden territory until it had culminated a minute ago with her lips an inch from his and him trying to get her to run away with him.

Cindy deserved every happiness in the world. She was a kind, generous, warm, wonderful woman. She deserved a man who was all those things, too. Yet throughout history it seemed to be the same. Women were attracted to the wrong men, to men who weren't good for them. To men who were not men at all, but monsters masquerading as men. He was one of those and even though Cindy didn't know it, she must sense it somehow and she was becoming attracted to it.

He tried to tell himself that it was just the stress of the moment, the shock and the danger, but he suspected that it ran deeper than that. In case it did, he owed it to her to leave. If he cared for her that was what he would do, even if the thought nearly destroyed him. It was the right thing to do. It was what he had to do. Because he knew in his heart that if he stayed eventually being that close to her would wear down his resistance. One day he would kiss her. Then, heaven help them both, he would never stop.

He heard footsteps and for a moment thought Cindy might be returning. These steps were too heavy, though. He closed his eyes, steeling himself for whatever was coming next.

It had taken all of his willpower to let Hank tie his wrists instead of punching the man and making a run for it. That would have resulted in a lot more injury, and possibly death, though, and if he did that he'd never be able to prove his innocence to anyone, not even Cindy even though she seemed predisposed to believe in him.

He opened his eyes and turned just as a figure stepped through the canvas into the wagon. It was Mark and the detective was staring at him with eyes that seemed to burn right through him.

"You've got the wrong man," Jeremiah said.

"Don't lie to me. After all this time, I finally know who you really are."

15

Mark stared at Jeremiah. The rabbi met his eyes, coolly. "And who am I?" he asked.

"You're a killer."

"So, you told everyone out there."

"So, I'm telling you. Look, what I said out there was true. I know that you killed that serial killer. I knew it then, I just couldn't prove it. And, frankly, I didn't want to press the issue too hard."

"There were a lot of police around that day. And, if I'm not mistaken, he was shot by one of them."

"No, he was shot by one of their guns. But I think you were the man holding it."

"You have no proof of that."

"No, and I never will at this point. All that was important back then was that the man was stopped. Besides, even if I could have proven my suspicions it would have been a clear case of either self defense or defense of others depending exactly on how it went down. Then there was that assassin at the kid's camp."

"Man was killed by a mountain lion," Jeremiah said, face still completely passive, revealing nothing.

"And I'm betting the Honolulu police have found a few bodies, or at least filed a few missing persons reports from when Cindy was kidnapped and you were over there rescuing her."

Mark pulled a pen and a piece of paper out of his shirt pocket and scribbled something on it.

"You're never going to pin these murders on me," Jeremiah said.

Mark passed him the note.

I'm pretty sure there's someone outside listening, Jeremiah read silently.

"Don't be too sure of that," Mark said.

Any idea who? Jeremiah barely managed to scribble with his hands tied the way they were.

"I'm too smart for you," Jeremiah said, his voice suddenly sounding harsh, sneering.

Mark read the note and shook his head.

"We'll see about that," Mark said, exiting abruptly.

He shoved his way through the canvas and then jumped down from the wagon. Liz was standing there, arms crossed. She looked slightly startled at his sudden appearance, but no more than could be expected.

"No visitors for the prisoner," Mark growled.

She lifted an eyebrow. "I just need my makeup kit. It's in there. Kyle wants to do a close-up."

Mark laughed. "And just how does he plan on doing that with all the cameras out of commission?"

"Norman and Hank both had personal handheld cameras in their bags. Clearly he didn't know about them. Anyway, they've offered to take some footage to salvage what they can...or to at least have something to show on the news when word of all this gets out."

Mark managed to contain his disappointment. "Okay, grab it, but be quick," he said. "And don't get too close to him, he's dangerous," he added. He shook his head in frustration. Kyle was unbelievable if he was still trying to salvage this trip.

She was quick, returning less than ten seconds later lugging the giant case.

"You need help getting it down?" he offered.

"No, I've got it," she said, jumping down off the wagon and hauling the heavy case down afterward.

He waited until she was headed over to where the others were grouped, rolling the case behind her, before he took a quick look around the other side of the wagon. Satisfied that Jeremiah was isolated for the time being he went over to rejoin the group where he could keep an eye on everyone. There were eight suspects in total, counting the missing Roddy, and it would be a lot easier to keep an eye on all of them if he could enlist some help from Traci, Cindy, or even Cindy's brother.

He and Jeremiah had agreed, though, that for their plan to make the killer let down his guard to work everyone had to be completely convincing in their reactions to him accusing Jeremiah. He felt bad about not telling Traci and Cindy the truth, but neither of them was actress enough to have faked the reactions they gave earlier. Since most of the suspects were television people, it would likely have been easy for the killer to spot a bad acting job.

As it was he had nearly lost himself in his own role, bringing up everything that had ever bothered him about Jeremiah or stood out as odd. By the time he'd finished he'd all but convinced himself that Jeremiah really was the killer. As it was, there was still a tiny doubt in the back of his mind. *Masquerading as the killer to flush out the killer would be perfect cover if he actually was the killer.* He shook his head and told himself he was being paranoid again. It was turning into a bad habit.

As he joined the group Traci glared at him, while Cindy just looked straight ahead. There was going to be hell to pay with both of them later, but if they caught a killer before anyone else died it would be worth it.

"We only have permission from the land owner to move the herd through this particular area, not leave it here for even a day or two no matter the circumstances. Our obligation to our employer and the legal contracts he's signed require us to keep moving the herd as planned," Zack was saying.

Curly was nodding, backing him up. Given that it was their comrade who was dead it gave more weight to their argument.

"Now, we've only got four days left before we reach Righteousness, the town where we drop you all off. We can't trust our prisoner on a horse so we can only travel as fast as the chuck wagon anyway. It only makes sense to see this through."

It was still a weird sounding name for a town to him. Then again he had once driven through Bacon, Texas and Traci had an uncle who lived in Toad Suck, Arkansas, so compared to those Righteousness didn't seem so bad.

"We should send someone ahead, alert the local authorities. Maybe they can start trying to find the body," Norman said.

"Oh no, I'm not splitting up the group again," Kyle said. "Look what happened the last time we sent someone ahead for help."

"But now that we've caught the killer-" Norman began.

"It won't matter. Whoever killed Tex would have buried him. And if not, buzzards will get to him long before anyone could ever find a body out here," Hank said.

"Okay, so, we're going to stay together and finish this thing," Kyle said, his face grim.

"It's not going to hurt your ratings any," someone in the crowd muttered.

"Who said that?" Kyle asked, face draining of color.

No one moved.

"This is a tragedy. What happens with the show is ultimately the network's call. It's our duty, though, to continue to roll footage just in case we don't have the right killer or he has an accomplice. That way the police can go through it if need be."

"Oh, we have the right killer," Mark said with all the confidence he could muster.

Kyle looked at him. "I trust your judgment, but I still hope you're wrong. The man did save my sister's life."

More times than you can even count, buddy, Mark thought to himself.

"So, we all have a job to do," Kyle continued. "I suggest we do it to the best of our abilities."

He turned and stalked off. The rest of them began to disperse and he noticed Liz standing there with her makeup case.

"Guess Kyle changed his mind about that close-up," Mark said.

"Typical," she said with a sigh. "He changes his mind every fifteen minutes on a good day."

She walked away slowly, trailing the case behind.

Mark turned and found Traci in his face, her eyes blazing. He took an involuntary step backward.

"How could you?" she seethed.

"Shouldn't you be asking him that?" Mark said with a straight face although he inwardly winced. Her current anger was nothing compared to what it was going to be later when she learned how he had tricked her along with everyone else.

Cindy was quiet and he hated to think what had to be going through her mind. She was probably reliving every experience the two of them had shared, wondering what exactly he had done that she had never been aware of. He wouldn't trade places with her for anything, but thanks to what had happened with Paul he more than understood.

At least she'd only have to wonder for a few hours, maybe a day or two. He was beginning to think he was going to be left wondering for the rest of his life.

"We need to get packed up so we can get out of here," he said, more gruffly than he had intended.

Traci bent down and scooped the contents of Jeremiah's backpack back into it, including carefully wrapping the knife back up and putting it in. When Mark raised an eyebrow she just looked at him.

"Where else am I going to put it right now?" she snapped.

She had a point. At the moment nowhere was safe for something like that, especially with a killer still on the loose.

When she was finished she and Cindy moved over and started rolling up their sleeping bags. After a moment Mark headed for his as well. His mind was still racing, though.

Currently his money was on either Wayne or Junior or both. He just needed one of them to slip up now that Jeremiah was tied up in the chuck wagon. So, while he rolled up his sleeping bag and finished gathering together his gear he kept a watchful eye on everyone else.

The others were busy packing up, too, except for Kyle. Kyle had been standing by himself for a while, hands in his pockets, clearly thinking hard about something. As Mark watched, Kyle suddenly moved, heading in the direction of the chuck wagon. He guessed that the television host was heading in to have a talk with the man who he thought was trying to kill him.

Jeremiah looked up as Kyle entered the wagon. He was actually a little surprised to see him, but he steeled himself to answer the other's questions.

"Why are you trying to kill me?" Kyle asked without preamble. "What did I ever do to you?"

"You've done plenty to Cindy," Jeremiah said sarcastically.

Kyle shook his head. "I don't buy it. Sure, we see things differently and we don't get along, but that's no reason for you to try and kill me."

Jeremiah knew he had to maintain his cover. There was no telling if anyone else could hear them. Besides, letting Kyle in on the plan was not going to happen. So, Jeremiah leaned forward and dropped his voice slightly so that it was rougher sounding.

"The real question is, why weren't you man enough to admit up front what type of trip this was and that you would be filming the whole thing?"

"I was afraid Cindy wouldn't come, obviously. She's not exactly the on-camera type of personality. But, honestly, why should that even matter? She's handling it just fine, like I knew she would."

"Not everyone wants their face plastered across television sets all over the country and computer screens all over the world," Jeremiah growled.

"Come on, what possible harm could there be?"

"Think real hard about why someone wouldn't want their face seen that way," Jeremiah said, his voice even lower and dripping with menace.

"I would imagine only a criminal wouldn't-" Kyle stopped talking abruptly, his eyes growing round. "What did you do?" he asked.

Jeremiah smirked. "Take a wild guess."

Kyle took a step back, nearly tripping over some of the boxes stacked behind him. "Why, why didn't you just back out of the trip when you realized what was happening?"

"And tell Cindy what exactly about my reasons for doing so?"

Kyle lifted a shaking hand. "You, you stay away from my sister."

"Look who decided to play the loving brother role. You know, Kyle, it doesn't really suit you."

"I'm serious, don't you touch her."

"You mean, more than I already have?" Jeremiah pushed. "She's so sweet and soft and trusting. You want to know what it feels like when she's in my arms, whispering all her secrets to me?"

"I won't hear another word!" Kyle shouted as he left.

Jeremiah smiled to himself. He had agitated Kyle enough that the other would no longer question his guilt at all.

Cindy had just finished rolling up her sleeping bag and securing it when Kyle came over to her, face flushed.

"You need to stay away from him, he's trouble," Kyle said, voice shaking.

"Who, Jeremiah?" Cindy asked, wondering who else he could possibly be referencing.

"Yes, he's bad news."

"I think you and Mark are wrong about him being the killer," Cindy said. "You don't know Jeremiah like I do."

"No, you don't know him at all. Trust me, I just got a glimpse of the real him and it's terrible. He's a criminal, Cindy, and you need to get as far away from him as fast as possible."

"I'll do no such thing," Cindy said, lifting her chin defiantly. "I believe in him. He's a good man."

"Why are women always so blinded by love?" Kyle ranted. "None of you can ever see straight when it comes to looking at the guy you've given your heart to."

"I'm not in love with him! He's my friend, and I'm going to stand by him because that's what friends do. And if you ever had a true friend in your life and not just coworkers and schmoozers you would understand that," she lashed back.

"That's enough!" Traci snapped. "Both of you. Bickering among ourselves won't help anything. Now I have a hard time believing Jeremiah did this, but it looks bad, and we have to be objective about this and brace ourselves for the worst. If he didn't do it, though, then we need to remain focused and remember that whoever did could strike again at any time. So, just lay off each other, okay?"

Kyle turned and stormed away.

"Thanks," Cindy muttered.

"I meant it. It does look bad, you have to be prepared in case he did do this."

Cindy shook her head. "Not Jeremiah."

Traci rolled her eyes. "Please, if half of what Mark said really is true then what you should be asking is 'Why not Jeremiah?' You know I'm right."

Cindy bit her tongue. It would do no good to antagonize Traci, too, particularly when she could use her help finding the real killer.

Twenty minutes later everyone was packed up and gear was stowed with Jeremiah in the back of the chuck wagon. Mark handled putting everything away, insisting that the prisoner was too dangerous for others to go near. That just infuriated Cindy more, but she still managed to hold her tongue.

Zack approached her a minute later, his face worried. "How's your ankle?" he asked without preamble.

"It just twinges now, but I'm not looking forward to getting on a horse," she admitted.

"Well, you might not have to. See, we do have a bit of a problem. We need someone to take over driving the wagon."

"I don't know how," she said.

"No, but you watched Brent do it for a day and a half and it only took me a couple of hours to teach him. Neither Curly nor I can do it because we need to stick with the herd and the others. So, if I sit with you for the first hour or so, do you think you can try to take it over?"

"I'll try," she said, her nervousness actually overshadowed by her excitement. It could prove to be her chance to help Jeremiah.

"Great. Everyone else is getting ready, so I think we should go ahead and get started."

Cindy climbed up into the wagon eagerly and took her place in the driver's seat. Zack got up beside her and handed her the reins.

"Okay, show me what to do," she said doggedly.

Mark was a little surprised that Cindy had agreed to learn how to drive the team of horses pulling the wagon. He knew she wasn't eager to get back up on a horse, but he suspected that her willingness to drive the wagon actually had everything to do with being close to Jeremiah.

Whatever the reason at least he was reasonably certain the two of them were out of harm's way. He just wished he could say so for the rest of them. With Zack's help he had wrapped Brent's body in a tarp and stored it in the wagon. He hated to make Jeremiah ride with a dead man, but there was no way around it.

Curly held his horse for him while he mounted up. Soon the rest of them were on horseback as well.

He urged his mount into a trot, and headed out toward the herd. This was ridiculous. They should leave the herd behind, but hopefully opportunities would abound to catch the real killer.

Half the herd was laying down resting when they reached it. After a couple of minutes they had the animals up and moving. It was going to be another long day of stress and dust. He tried to hold back slightly so that he could keep an eye out for everyone else. Unfortunately, that meant eating even more of the herd's dust.

Tahiti. That's where he and Traci were going when all of this was over. Nothing bad ever happened there, he was sure of it.

Curly and Wayne were toward the front of the herd with Junior and Liz behind them a little ways. Right in front of him on the flanks were Hank and Norman, both dutifully filming while also trying to control their horses. Hank was doing a much better job of that than Norman whom Mark was certain was about to fall off his animal on more than one occasion. Traci was to his right, also clearly trying to keep everyone else in her sight.

They had been in motion for about a minute when there was a sudden commotion up ahead. He heard a high-pitched scream and Liz's horse reared up. Cattle scattered every which way and Curly turned back, racing his horse toward the source of the problem.

The hair on the back of Mark's neck stood on end. Something was very wrong. He saw Zack leap off the chuck wagon and hastily untie his horse from the back of the wagon and a moment later he, too, was racing toward Liz.

He heard shouts as Curly reached her first. Almost as though in a trance Mark kicked his horse forward. Something was happening and as much as he knew he wanted to steer clear he also knew that somehow it was going to be important to see what was going on.

Liz was still struggling to get her horse under control. She managed to bring the animal to a standstill just as Mark reached her. She, on the other hand, looked like she was going to be ill.

He turned and saw what had caused all the stir.

In the midst of the cattle, on the ground, was a pile of bloody rags. He blinked, struggling to comprehend what he was seeing. Then it finally hit him. He wasn't looking at a pile of clothes. He was looking at a mangled corpse.

They had finally found Roddy.

16

Cindy felt a thrill of victory as she managed to bring the horses and wagon to a stop all by herself after Zack leapt off. She swiveled in her seat, trying to see what was causing all the commotion.

"What's going on?" Jeremiah called from inside the wagon.

"I don't know," she said. "Liz's horse is freaking out or at least he was a second ago. Everyone's staring at something on the ground."

"I wonder what they found."

She stood up, trying to get a better view. "I just can't see."

"Someone should let us know soon enough."

This was her opportunity, Cindy realized. Everyone else was preoccupied. The extra horses were tied to the back of the wagon. She could cut Jeremiah loose and send him on his way while noone was looking.

You could go with him.

She flushed as the thought ambushed her. She firmly dismissed it from her mind, though. Someone had to stay behind to find the real killer and prove Jeremiah's innocence. If they both ran there would be noone to do that.

She quickly tied the reins so that the horses wouldn't move and she'd be able to easily retrieve them again. Then she climbed into the back.

"It doesn't sound good out there," Jeremiah commented.

She shook her head. She could hear shouting, but she couldn't make out what anyone was saying. She looked quickly around for one of the knives Brent must have had with him.

"What are you doing?" Jeremiah asked softly.

"I'm going to cut you free. This is your chance to escape."

"I'm not going to run," he said.

She looked up at him. He was staring at her, a half smile on his face.

"Why, those people out there, some of them are crazy. I don't know what they might try to do to you before we can get to a town."

"It's okay."

"No, it's not," she said, fear rushing through her. There was something wrong in his entire demeanor. He seemed too calm.

Too resigned, she realized.

"Listen to me," she said, grabbing his shoulders and shaking him. "You can't give up. You have to fight. We've been in lots of worse places than this. I'm not going to let anything happen to you, but you have to help me out."

"I appreciate what you're trying to do, but I think everything is going to work out just fine," he said earnestly.

She stared at him, wondering what had happened in the last little while to make him change his mind about running.

"Someone's coming," he said.

She turned and scrambled back out onto the wagon seat, grabbing for the reins as she looked back toward the herd.

Traci was riding up. She pulled her horse to a halt. "Did you hear?"

"No, I can't tell what's going on," Cindy said, struggling to control her agitation.

"They found Roddy, dead."

"Dead?" Cindy asked, sitting up straighter. He had been the one unknown, the one suspect she couldn't keep an eye on, and she felt completely terrible as she felt a twinge of relief to know that there wasn't someone unseen stalking them. "What happened?"

"Zack and Mark are trying to figure that out. He was trampled by the cattle, that's probably why noone could find him. I got a glimpse, it's really bad...not a whole lot left."

"So, did the cattle kill him or did a person?"

Traci blinked. "You think one of the animals could have killed him?"

"Well, I know there is a rather nasty steer in the group who attacked Curly. Or he could have tripped, been injured, and just stepped on one too many times."

"Okay, I'm no longer sure which scenario freaks me out more, killed by a person or killed by the animals," Traci said, her face turning ashen.

"Sorry," Cindy muttered. A moment later, though, she lit up. "If he was killed by the killer, then Jeremiah is innocent."

"How do you figure that?" Traci asked.

"Jeremiah was working on Brent when Kyle sent Roddy to find Zack."

"True, but we know that Roddy never found Zack. We also know that Jeremiah went out looking for Roddy.

Maybe he found him and killed him while Roddy was still trying to figure out where the doctor was."

Cindy felt as though she had been slapped. "You can't possibly believe Jeremiah did this."

Traci shook her head grimly. "I don't want to believe it, but frankly at the moment I'm just scared and confused about the whole thing."

"You don't have to be scared. We'll find the real killer and we'll make it out of this okay, you'll see."

"That's easy for you to say."

Cindy shook her head in amazement. "It's not easy for me to say. It comes from experience, lots of it, with finding killers with Jeremiah and Mark. I know that it's going to work out alright, I feel it." She took a deep breath. "Besides, God's not going to let me die on a cattle drive with my brother. It would just be wrong."

"Wrong? It would be wrong?" Traci asked incredulously. "Because everything else that's happened so far hasn't been wrong?"

"It's not that, it's just...complicated," Cindy said. "I just don't believe this is the end God has in store for us."

"It must be nice to be that confident," Traci said with a sigh. She turned and looked back over her shoulder. "I wonder how long it's going to take them to try and figure out what happened to him?" she said.

"I don't know. Crime scene units normally take forever, but that's in a house or a building or something. Out here? Plus it's not like they can dust for fingerprints or anything like that."

What Cindy didn't say was that she was hoping they would be on the move again shortly. Every hour delayed was an hour they were all trapped together in the middle of nowhere. She was becoming more convinced that reaching civilization in one piece was going to be harder than any of them thought.

She stood up and craned her neck. She still couldn't see the body, and from Traci's description, she was glad. Zack and Mark appeared to be off their horses while Curly and Hank were busy pushing cattle away from where they were, probably trying to give them as much room to work as possible.

She felt her stomach churn just at the thought of what they were looking at. At the same time she wished she could remember exactly who might have had the opportunity to kill Roddy while the rest of them were all gathered around Brent and Jeremiah. The only ones she knew for sure hadn't been present were the cowboys.

She swung around in her seat and poked her head through the canvas. "They found Roddy's body," she told Jeremiah.

"I heard. Sounds gruesome."

"What do you think of the three cowboys?" she asked.

"What do you mean?"

"They're the only ones I know for a fact weren't there when the rest of us were gathered around Brent's body. One of them could easily have killed Roddy."

"I don't think it could have been Zack," Traci spoke up.

Cindy turned to look at her. Traci had moved her horse in closer to participate in the conversation.

"Why not?" Jeremiah called out.

"There simply wasn't enough time between Roddy being sent out to find him and him arriving, especially if Roddy was killed in the middle of the herd and that's why noone could find him. Zack ran up on foot just a minute or so after Roddy left. Not enough time."

"She's right," Jeremiah said.

"Which leaves Tex and Curly," Cindy said.

"One of whom is dead," Traci noted.

"At least, we assume he is. We don't know for a fact that it was his blood. It could have even been an animal's blood, used to make us think he was dead," Jeremiah pointed out.

Cindy shuddered. Once again they were back to the possibility that the killer was out there, unseen. She didn't like it, but she had to admit that at this point without a body they had no proof that Tex was actually dead.

"Why would Tex want Kyle dead, though? Or Curly either, for that matter?" Traci asked.

Cindy snorted. "I think you're the only one here who actually likes my brother."

Traci's eyes narrowed. "He's a nice guy, you should get to know him more."

"We can argue my brother's merits later," Cindy said impatiently. "You're right, though, there's no obvious reason for either of them to want him dead whereas some of his coworkers have much more obvious motives."

"How about money?" Jeremiah spoke up.

"What about money?" Cindy asked.

"It's possible that whoever the killer is, one of the cowboys, one of the crew, that they're just the hired help so to speak and they're just doing it because someone else is paying them."

Cindy felt a headache coming on. "You mean, I might need to ask Kyle if *anyone anywhere* hates him enough to have him killed?"

"It's either that or continue to try to figure out who had the opportunity to commit each of the crimes," Traci said.

"Well, for Brent, I think it could have actually been anyone. Just about everyone was in the wagon at some point grabbing gear or putting stuff away. And since we have no idea when they actually poisoned the truffle salt, it will be impossible to narrow that one down," Cindy said.

"I've been thinking about Martin from the bunkhouse," Traci said, visibly shuddering. "Anyone in there could have killed him if it was truly murder and not just an accident."

"But the cowboys weren't in the bunkhouse with us," Cindy pointed out.

"Aaron was, though, and he went home straight away," Jeremiah said. "It's possible whoever was in charge pulled him out after he missed his target. Or, it's possible he is the one in charge and he removed himself to avoid suspicion."

"Is it possible one of the cowboys snuck into the bunkhouse and killed Martin?" Traci asked.

"I've been thinking about that," Jeremiah said, "but then I remembered how loudly the door to the cabin squeaked. They couldn't have gotten in that way without waking someone up I think."

"Maybe they woke up Martin," Cindy said darkly.

"I think there was a window in the bathroom. Someone might have come in through there," Traci said.

"And they could have left the same way," Jeremiah finished.

"Okay, again we really have no way of narrowing our suspect pool down," Cindy said irritated.

"And we can't prove that what happened to your saddle was anything more than an accident," Jeremiah pointed out. "If it wasn't, that would seem to incriminate one of the cowboys since it was their job to saddle the horses, but truly in all the chaos of getting started, anyone could have tampered with that saddle."

Cindy was beginning to think this mystery was the toughest they'd ever faced despite the fact that on the surface they had very few possible suspects. She sighed and craned her neck again to look over at Mark and Zack. They were on the ground now, clearly examining something, but her view was still obscured.

"So really that leaves us with Roddy and Tex. The only possible people who were out of eyesight of everyone else who might have had a shot at Roddy were Tex and Curly."

"And Jeremiah, he went out looking for him," Traci pointed out.

"Thanks for the vote of confidence," Jeremiah said, a dusting of sarcasm in his voice.

Traci shrugged even though Jeremiah couldn't see the gesture from where he was in the wagon.

"Hank also helped search. It's possible Roddy was lost or injured at that point which was why he hadn't yet returned to the wagon."

"Okay, so we're all agreed that it had to be Tex, Curly, Jeremiah or Hank who killed Roddy, right?" Traci asked.

"Unless it was the steer or the other cattle," Cindy said.

"Or Aaron or someone else who has been following us," Jeremiah interjected.

Traci groaned. "This detective stuff is harder than it looks."

Cindy laughed grimly. "It is at that. Okay, let's take a look at Tex. Who had access to him after he left the camp?

"Noone, he was headed away from camp, the cattle, everything," Traci said.

"Immediately after he left Zack and Curly saddled up to go check on the cattle," Jeremiah said. "It's possible that one of them actually rode out and headed Tex off."

"But we know that Tex's horse was faster than Curly's," Cindy protested.

"Not if Curly was running his horse out flat to catch him and Tex was going at a reasonable pace," Traci said.

"But this could bring Zack also back under suspicion, especially if Roddy's death was an accident," Cindy said.

"You're both forgetting one thing," Jeremiah said.

"What?" Cindy and Traci asked in unison.

"Anyone could have killed Tex, if he circled back and was waiting to meet with someone."

"Two killers?" Cindy asked in a whisper.

"It's happened before," Jeremiah said.

"It would explain a lot," Traci replied.

"That's it, I definitely have a headache," Cindy said, pressing her fingertips into her forehead.

"I'm pretty sure I'm getting one, too," Traci said. "How do we prove any of this?"

"We wait, we watch. Sooner or later the killer will slip up," Cindy said. "I mean, just think about how jittery we all are. The killer has to be a thousand times more so wondering if they're going to get caught and knowing they still haven't accomplished their goal of killing Kyle."

"If that truly was their goal," Jeremiah pointed out. "For all we know they wanted Brent and Roddy dead for some reason and Kyle is a red herring."

"If that's true, Kyle could even be a suspect," Traci said, her voice strained sounding.

Cindy rolled her eyes. "My brother might be a lot of things, but he's not a killer."

"Honestly, I'm not sure we can rule out the possibility," Traci said. "I mean, the two of you aren't close, you don't really speak, how do you know what kind of person he's become since you were kids?"

The thought chilled Cindy to the bone. She didn't want to even contemplate it as a possibility. "But even if he did want them both dead for some reason, why kill them now? It's sabotaging his own show."

"Or giving it stellar ratings for when it does finally air because of all the tragedy surrounding it," Jeremiah suggested.

"No, I refuse to believe my brother is that psycho and that shallow," she said. "That just doesn't make sense to me."

A moment later she saw Mark stand up and get back on his horse. He trotted over toward them and she realized she was holding her breath as she waited to hear the news. When he reached them, his face was grim.

"Traci said you found Roddy's body," Cindy said.

"What's left of it. There was barely enough to recognize."

She cringed at the thought and tried not to let her imagination run wild picturing the scene.

"I need to get a tarp so we can wrap up the remains and take them with us," he said.

"I'll get it," Cindy said, turning and pushing through the canvas into the back of the wagon.

She stopped in surprise. Jeremiah was standing up, his hands completely unbound. He looked at her and lifted a finger in front of his lips to indicate that she should be quiet.

She nodded slowly.

He turned to rummage in a pile of things, and then produced a tarp which he handed her. She bit back the urge to say "thank you" as she turned and headed back to the front of the wagon.

Once there she handed the tarp to Mark who had difficulty angling his horse closer. The animal skittered, sidestepping quite a few times and Mark started muttering under his breath. He finally got close enough to grab the tarp from her and she sat back down on the bench.

"Could you tell if he was killed by someone or just gored or trampled to death?" she asked.

He shook his head. "No, and to be honest, I'm not sure anyone's going to be able to figure that out with certainty. Like I said, it's a real mess. You ladies should stay here until we get it cleaned up."

"How are the others holding up?" Traci asked quietly.

Mark shrugged. "About as well as can be expected, some better than others."

"Do any of them look guilty?" Cindy asked, cutting to the chase.

"At this point everyone looks guilty to me," Mark said rolling his eyes. "This whole thing is a complete mess."

Cindy noted that he didn't instantly revert to blaming Jeremiah. That had to be a good thing, but she refrained from pointing it out.

"Maybe you should send everyone who's not helping you over this way," Traci suggested. "That way they're not in the way and we can talk to them and see if we can draw any conclusions," Traci said.

"Seems like a good idea," Mark agreed. "I'll send them over pronto."

And despite all the death and craziness Cindy watched as Traci smiled.

"What?" Mark asked, obviously noticing his wife's expression.

"You're starting to sound like a cowboy," she said, and even Cindy could hear the admiration in her voice.

She glanced at Mark and couldn't tell if he was pleased or dismayed. He spun his horse, kicked him into motion and rode quickly back to the others. Cindy bit her lip. He had clearly been showing off for Traci. It was nice to see the two of them flirting with each other despite the years of marriage and the horror that they found themselves enmeshed in.

"He really is so handsome," Traci said softly.

"His riding's getting a lot better," Cindy said.

"I noticed."

Mark reached the group and they watched as he handed the tarp down to Zack. He then started gesturing back toward the wagon and after a few seconds the film crew trotted their horses toward them. They all looked weary and a bit shell shocked.

Liz in particular was riding strangely, kind of flopping around in the saddle.

"Is she okay?" Cindy asked.

"She certainly doesn't look okay," Traci noted.

They both watched as the riders approached. Cindy tried hard to study their faces. Kyle, in particular, looked sort of hollow while a couple of the others looked numb. She couldn't read Wayne's expression at all. She turned her attention back to Liz.

The woman was riding even worse, sagging forward a bit over the saddle. “I think something is seriously wrong with her,” Cindy said, alarmed.

“I think you’re right,” Traci said, voice tight.

A moment later Traci exclaimed, “Look, her eyes are closed!”

They were.

Seconds later Liz’s horse stopped a few feet shy of the others. Liz swayed for a moment in the saddle.

“Liz, are you okay?” Cindy shouted.

A moment later Liz tumbled to the ground.

17

Traci screamed and Cindy jumped down from the wagon before she even knew what she was doing. She raced to Liz's side. Liz's horse shied away at Cindy's approach and Kyle caught its bridle as it tried to run past him.

Cindy hit her knees and the first thing she noticed was that Liz was breathing.

"She's alive!" she shouted up at Traci.

She stared back down at Liz, not knowing what else she could do for her. She was afraid to even lift her head off the ground in case she'd injured her neck or back in the fall.

"Get Zack," she said, looking up, trying not to think about how this was so similar to when Brent had collapsed. She heard someone shouting for the doctor and she just kept watching Liz's face, searching for the slightest sign of movement.

Suddenly, the woman's eyelashes flickered and a moment later she opened her eyes and looked up at Cindy with a bewildered expression. "What happened?" she asked.

"You fell off your horse. It looked like you lost consciousness first," Cindy explained. "Are you in pain?"

"No, not really. I mean I feel a little sore."

"I don't doubt it, you hit the ground pretty hard."

"We were coming back over to the wagon and I felt a little dizzy and lightheaded and that's the last thing I remember," Liz said. "I get low blood sugar sometimes. I brought a package of juice boxes with me just in case. They should be in a cooler somewhere in the wagon."

"I'll go get one," Cindy said, scrambling to her feet just as Zack arrived, face pale.

She could swear she heard him mutter something under his breath about things being worse than they had been in the army. She had a hard time believing that, but she didn't comment as she turned to the wagon. She climbed up into the back and Jeremiah regarded her with raised brows.

"Liz fainted. It looks like her blood sugar might have crashed."

"Could also be stress. She was the one who screamed when the body was found, yes?"

"That's right," Cindy said. "Where's the cooler?"

Jeremiah pointed and Cindy opened it. She pushed aside several packets of frozen meat and found a package of juice boxes just like Liz had said. One of them was already missing. Cindy wondered if Liz had already had an attack on the trip as she grabbed another one of the boxes and moved the meat back into position.

She scrambled back down from the wagon and headed back over to Liz. Zack was checking her over and she handed the juice box to him. He helped Liz sit up and she began to drink a minute later.

"She'll be fine in a few minutes," Zack reassured everyone present.

All around heads bobbed up and down. People were beyond words, they were too tired, too shocked.

Cindy went back and rejoined Traci next to the wagon. The other woman was rubbing her arms repetitively and her eyes were still wide.

"You okay?" Cindy asked.

"Yeah, it's just a lot, you know?"

Cindy understood all too well. She was just grateful this latest incident had nothing to do with foul play.

Mark's nerves and patience were both wearing thin. He was at the point that he wanted to arrest the entire camera crew and the cowboys and throw them in the back of the wagon. If he had thought he, Jeremiah, Cindy and Traci could successfully transport all of them to Righteousness in that manner he would do it in a heartbeat. It wasn't practical, though. That would be three days of guarding people, at least one of whom would be growing increasingly desperate. Then there was the matter of even figuring out where they were headed. If one or both of the cowboys did turn out to be involved they couldn't be trusted to send them on the quickest path or even the correct one.

No, as much as he didn't like it they were just going to have to stick to the plan and wait things out, hoping the killer would trip themselves up. If nothing happened in the next day, though, he was thinking they were going to have to do something to force the issue. He wasn't sure how long they could survive on the trail without someone else falling victim. He and Jeremiah were going to have to have a talk later. He needed to talk with Traci and Cindy, too. Between the four of them they should be able to figure this out.

The more Jeremiah thought about it the more suspicious he became of Norman. Norman was the most unassuming of their seven suspects and he had come late to the party. Neither of those, though, ruled him out. He had arrived awfully quickly and conveniently on the scene to take over for the dead Martin. This was supposed to be Norman's show, his baby. Instead of getting to host, he wasn't even allowed to be the cinematographer on the show. Killing Martin allowed him to take over that position and gain a place on the crew. In his twisted mind he probably thought that killing Kyle would allow him to move into the position of host that should have been his.

If Norman believed Kyle had stolen his show that could cause enough hatred to be reason enough to murder him. If Norman thought getting Kyle out of the way would allow him to get his show back, that could also be reason enough to murder him. What better way of throwing suspicion off himself than by supposedly not even being there during the first murder?

He might not even have been, that was the beauty of it. He could have paid Tex to do it for him. Then he could have later killed Tex either because he didn't want someone else around who knew the truth or because Tex tried to blackmail him. It was a good plan. Who knew if it would have worked if he had managed to kill Kyle either with the saddle or the poison and it had been attributed to an accident. It would have become the ill-fated show on which two people died. That kind of thing could certainly drive ratings from curiosity seekers.

Roddy could have easily overheard something from Norman or Tex necessitating that one of them kill him. That is, if it hadn't been an accident, which Jeremiah very much doubted.

He would have to discuss his theory with Mark. Norman was the logical killer. He had the strongest motive and, hypothetically, the most to gain. Maybe working together they could set a trap for Norman.

It really was the most logical explanation. He could tell that Wayne hated Kyle, but he didn't think the man would resort to premeditated murder. Kill Kyle in a fistfight in the heat of the moment maybe, but plan it out, Jeremiah didn't think so. Junior wasn't likely to try something like that on his own. With his personality he was far more likely to be an accomplice than a mastermind. There was a slim chance Junior was working for Norman, but Jeremiah's money was on Tex as the accomplice.

Zack and Hank he had pretty much ruled out. He had a hard time believing either of them was involved. Liz and Curly were both a bit more unknown, but he couldn't see any real motivation for either of them in either killing Kyle or shutting down the production. Besides, Curly had seemed genuinely distraught over the death of his friend.

With it settled in his mind all he had to do now was wait for an opportunity to speak to Mark alone. He hoped the detective would check in with him before they got started back on the trail. Twenty minutes later, though, it looked like that was not to be as he could hear Cindy and Zack taking their seats back at the front of the wagon again. Jeremiah sighed. Trapping Norman was just going to have to wait.

They were back on the trail and Zack was sitting next to Cindy again. Cindy was surprised at first that Liz had declined to ride on the wagon, but had chalked it up to not wanting to be too close to either the dead bodies or Jeremiah.

They had gone nearly half an hour in silence when Zack finally spoke. “You know, it’s the craziest thing, but I keep waiting for the next emergency,” he said. “I can feel the muscles in my legs all bunched up like I’m just waiting to leap down from the wagon again.”

“It’s not crazy,” Cindy reassured him. “I know exactly how you feel. Whenever I’m in the middle of something like this I feel the same way, like I’m just waiting to figure out which way to jump.”

“That’s it exactly! I don’t know how some people live their lives this way.”

“Like cops?” she asked.

“Yeah, and outlaws, too.”

“Outlaws?”

“Yeah, my great-great grandfather and his cousin were outlaws in the old west, they robbed banks and trains, that sort of thing. They actually had a hideout not that far from here.”

“Really?”

“Yeah, you see that mountain right over there with the sheer side facing us?” he asked, pointing off to the right and ahead of them slightly.

“Yeah.”

“There’s a cave at the base of it just around the side. It goes in for about a hundred feet, angles off to the right, and then dumps you into a little hidden valley. There’s still an old rundown cabin even. It’s actually ingenious, most people never think to go far enough into the cave to find the valley.”

“That’s cool. How do you know it’s there?”

"I've been a few times. The first time was when I was little. My grandfather took me."

"Does the land belong to your family?"

"No, they all moved out to northern California before my great grandfather was born, founded a nice little town."

"That's amazing. I don't even know my great-grandfather's first name let alone anything about where he lived or what he did for a living."

He shrugged. "Being connected to your past can be either a blessing or a curse."

That was certainly the way she felt about her own personal past sometimes, although it generally felt like more of a curse than a blessing.

After another few minutes Zack got back on his horse and left the team in her hands. She felt trepidation, but also a great deal of pride that he trusted her to drive the horses.

After a nerve-wracking couple of minutes she finally relaxed. She looked around, taking in the scenery. The mountain that hid the entrance to the secret outlaw hideout didn't seem to be that far away, but she wondered how close they'd get to it by the time they stopped for the night. She kind of wished she could actually see it.

From old west outlaws her mind drifted to modern day killers. She found herself running through the lists of suspects repeatedly, trying to view them from all different angles, trying to decide who had motive and opportunity and the willingness to carry out their plan. It would, of course, be ironic if it was Zack and what he'd said about the past being a curse or a blessing would carry extra weight.

She couldn't believe it was him, though. It just didn't fit with everything she'd seen of him so far. She finally ruled him out and let her mind continue working on the rest of the list.

After another hour she came to the conclusion that it had to be Norman. Norman could have easily been using Tex as an accomplice or Tex could have also been a helpless victim who stumbled onto the truth. Either way she was willing to bet Norman was involved.

When they stopped she'd share her thoughts with both Jeremiah and Mark. Hopefully one or both of them were thinking along the same lines as she was. Until then there was nothing to do really but just try to enjoy the moment.

Something she wasn't particularly good at.

Because of their late start they pushed on through lunch and when they stopped three hours later it was none too soon as far as Cindy was concerned. Her arms were aching from holding the reins and managing the team. It wasn't nearly as difficult as she had feared, but it was still exhausting work. After tying up the reins she stood and stretched and then climbed through into the back of the wagon.

"Food, finally. I think we'll be camping here tonight, too," she told Jeremiah.

"So I figured."

She did a double take as she realized that his hands were bound again. Nobody had been in the back of the wagon, though, except her. She met his eyes and he winked. He didn't want anyone to know he could free himself. She took a breath and nodded, indicating that she could play along.

"I think Norman did it," she whispered.

He nodded. "I came to the same conclusion."

"I keep feeling like there's something important I'm missing, though."

He frowned and shook his head. Apparently he wasn't feeling the same way. She sighed and turned to her work.

She grabbed some canned food and a pot and headed outside, grateful to see that Hank was already starting a cookfire.

"Thanks," she said as she walked up. Her and Jeremiah's certainty that Norman was the killer was already making her feel more relaxed toward the others. She just prayed they were right.

"We're stopping for the night," Mark said as he walked up a few minutes later. "Everyone's beyond exhausted and it makes no sense to eat and then clean up only to spend another hour or so on the trail before we have to stop and settle in before nightfall."

"Makes sense to me," she said. "Personally I'm ready to crash."

"Not before you finish dinner, please," he said with a groan.

She glanced around to see if anyone else could hear them before lowering her voice. "Jeremiah and I both think Norman is behind all this."

"You do, huh?" Mark asked, face inscrutable. "Well, I think I'm just going to go have a talk with Jeremiah. Let him out to walk around for a few minutes."

"I'm sure he'd appreciate that," Cindy said, trying not to betray what she knew about the fact that he could do that anytime he wanted.

"Okay, sounds like a plan," he said before heading off for the wagon. A minute later she saw him reappear with Jeremiah. The two walked off.

"Can I help?" Liz asked as she walked up.

"No, I think I've got it," Cindy said. "How are you feeling?"

"Better, mostly embarrassed."

Cindy waved her hand. "Don't worry about it, we're just glad you're okay."

"Me, too. I'm going to go grab myself another juice box just to be on the safe side. Do you need me to get you anything?"

"Actually, if you could grab some bottled water for everyone, that would be great."

"No problem."

Cindy had just about finished heating up the chili and corn when Liz returned, arms full of bottles. One slipped and fell on the ground.

"Dang it," Liz said with a sigh. "I should have just made two trips."

"It's okay," Cindy said with a smile as she stood and took some of the other bottles and put them on the ground. "Half the time in the grocery store I go in for one thing and end up at the register like this."

Liz laughed. "We should go shopping together sometime, see between the two of us how much we could juggle."

Cindy couldn't help but laugh at the image. "I can totally see that."

"Anything else I can do?"

Cindy winced. "Actually, yeah, we're also going to need plates."

"Not a problem. Where are they?"

Cindy described the location and a minute later Liz had returned.

"See, much more manageable when things stack properly," Liz said.

"But not nearly as fun."

Ten minutes later everyone descended on the fire, looking ragged and beyond exhausted. They had already grabbed their backpacks and sleeping bags and set up the basics for the sleeping area. She wouldn't be surprised if after dinner several of them headed right back there.

Everyone's ready to drop, Cindy thought as she passed out water and plates of food. She found herself looking longingly, though, at Liz's juice box, wishing she had a soda or something sweet to drink. She thought about asking Liz if she could swipe one of the juices, but she knew Liz would really need them if she had other sugar crashes like the one that morning.

She grabbed her food last and sat down on the ground with her plate on her knees and the water bottle beside her. Once there she picked at her food, realizing that even though she was physically spent she really wasn't that hungry. She was stressed out, though.

She glanced across the fire at Jeremiah seated beside Mark, struggling to eat with his hands tied together. She was grateful Mark had allowed him the ability to eat with the rest. Surprisingly no one else complained. Then again, no one was even really talking, just eating in silence.

The meal wasn't even over before Traci started yawning. Apparently it was contagious because within minutes it seemed everyone was.

"It's been a rough day," Mark finally said, breaking the silence. "I suggest we all get some rest."

He helped Jeremiah to his feet. "I'll be keeping one eye open," he advised him.

Cindy was surprised that Mark was going to let Jeremiah sleep outside and not in the wagon. Then again, there was no room to lie down in there, especially now with the two bodies taking up space.

Cindy got busy gathering up plates and scraping them off. “Let me help,” Liz said. Together they wiped each of them down quickly with a disinfectant wipe. They did the same for the pots and then Cindy took it all back and stored it in the wagon.

When she returned Liz was sitting next to the fire. Cindy sat down next to her, and picked up her unopened water bottle. Again she toyed with asking Liz for a juice, but she knew she needed to just tough it out. She could go without the sugar. She turned and noticed, startled, that everyone seemed to already be asleep. A couple of them were even lying on top of their sleeping bags still wearing the same clothes they’d been riding in. Even both cowboys were asleep.

I guess the herd’s quiet enough tonight they don’t have to worry. Either that or they just were too tired to care.

“That was...fast.”

“Yeah, I guess it’s been a hard day for all of us,” Liz said.

“I guess that means I’m taking first watch,” Cindy said.

Liz cocked her head to the side. “But, Jeremiah’s tied up, no one should have to stay up.”

“I still don’t think Jeremiah did it,” Cindy said firmly.

“That’s sweet of you to believe in your boyfriend like that,” Liz said.

“He is not my boyfriend. I don’t know why people keep thinking he is.”

Liz blinked at her. "It's the way you are together. You're obviously close, and you care a great deal for each other. Then there's the way that you look at him and he looks at you, like no one else in the world matters."

"I don't...he doesn't...you're crazy," Cindy finally sputtered.

Liz shrugged. "Maybe, but I know a thing or two about love and you two have definitely got it."

Cindy felt the heat rising in her cheeks and she dropped her eyes to the fire. "I-I don't know how I feel about him," she admitted at last.

I can't believe I'm doing this and with a complete stranger, she thought.

"Really, are you sure it's not more like you don't want to admit it because then you'll actually have to do something about it instead of letting things stay in a nice, safe little bubble like they are now?"

"I don't know," Cindy whispered.

"Look, you're never going to know what this thing between you could become if you don't take a risk."

"I'm sort of risk avoidant," Cindy admitted.

"Some risks are worth it. I know whereof I speak."

"It's too complicated."

"No, it's not. You're just making excuses."

Cindy sighed, wondering how she could explain everything she was thinking or feeling to Liz.

"I just don't know. What about tomorrow, what will happen then?" Cindy asked.

Liz sighed and lifted her juice box. "I propose a toast."

Cindy picked up her water bottle and screwed off the cap.

"To tomorrow, may it take care of itself and leave us in peace tonight."

Cindy tapped her water bottle against the juice box. Liz drank and Cindy sat, almost frozen, as she contemplated what Liz had said. Matthew 6:34 said something very similar. "Take therefore no thought for the morrow: for the morrow shall take thought for the things of itself. Sufficient unto the day is the evil thereof."

All her life she had let her fear of what might happen stop her from doing so many things. Had she let that fear stop her from truly living?

"Hello, earth to Cindy."

Cindy shook her head and turned to Liz. "Sorry, I was just thinking," she admitted as she set down her water. "Maybe you're right."

"I know I'm right."

"I just don't think I can say it out loud."

"Then write it down."

"I could never show it to him," Cindy said.

"Then just show it to yourself. Admit how you're feeling. I guarantee you'll feel better once you do."

"I don't have any paper," Cindy admitted.

"Here, I have some," Liz said, digging in her pocket and producing a paper and pen.

Cindy took them, remembering having glanced briefly at them when Mark had had her and Traci inspect the contents of everyone's pockets. She took the cap off the pen and set it down on the paper.

She took a deep breath. What she was about to do couldn't be undone. She felt terror and exhilaration all mixed up into one knot in the pit of her stomach. She stared at the paper, willing herself to do this.

The paper had a blue tinge to it and a faint scrollwork at the top. She had seen that scrollwork before. She blinked several times, thinking.

She had seen the scrollwork on the love letter Norman had been carrying with him. That letter had been written on one of Liz's pieces of paper.

Cindy looked sharply up at her. "Are you and Norman..."

She stopped as she stared at Liz. The other woman's face was contorted into a snarl. "Why couldn't you have been a good little girl and just chugged the dang water like everyone else?"

18

Cindy leaped to her feet and her eyes flicked over to the sleeping forms in horror as Liz's words sank in. "What have you done?" she shouted.

"Turns out the good doctor has all kinds of wonderful things in that bag. They'll be out for hours. Not you, though. You'll be dead. You and your brother."

Out for hours. Which meant help wouldn't be coming in time. Cindy's only chance was to subdue Liz. She thought of the rope binding Jeremiah's hands. First she'd have to knock her out, though.

Mark has a gun! she remembered at last. So did both of the cowboys. If only she could get to one of them.

Cindy's heart was hammering in her chest. She tried to dodge past Liz. The other woman yanked a knife out of her boot and slashed at Cindy.

Cindy screamed as the knife slashed across her chest. She scrambled backward, nearly falling into the fire.

"Kyle's not going anywhere. So as soon as I kill you I can finally take care of him."

"But why?" Cindy sobbed.

"Why do you think?" Liz hissed.

"Norman! He put you up to this!"

"No!" Liz shouted. "Norman could never even think of something like this. He's too nice, too sweet. He needed me to do this for him."

Liz lunged forward, swinging the knife and Cindy scrambled out of the way. She could feel blood dripping down her skin but she dare not look. She had to keep Liz away from Kyle and the others and keep from getting killed herself.

"I'll tell the authorities that you did it."

"And how do you plan to do that? You'll never make it to Righteousness."

Cindy was stepping carefully, rapidly swiveling her head to try and get a feel for the landscape. Then she saw Kyle's horse, Silver, just a short ways away. He was still wearing his saddle. A couple other horses farther away were, too. They were all grazing on the grass, oblivious to the human drama happening nearby. The starving cowboys had grabbed food before planning on taking care of the animals but had been drugged before they could.

Cindy turned and eyed Liz. "Care to bet on that?"

She turned and sprinted for all she was worth toward Silver. She heard a shout behind her but didn't look back. The massive white horse looked up as she approached, but didn't move away.

She grabbed the dangling reins, yanking them over his head and launched herself upward until she was laying across his back. She swung into the saddle and kicked her heels. He jumped and then kicked out as Liz got close to his hindquarters.

Out of the corner of her eye Cindy saw Liz go for one of the other horses just as she'd hoped she would. She needed to lead her away from the camp, keep her away until the others could wake up. Hopefully Jeremiah would figure out what had happened.

She clung to the pommel of the saddle for dear life as the great animal raced forward. The wind whipped at her face causing her eyes to tear. Strands of hair that had come free of her ponytail obscured her vision.

She had no idea how to get to Righteousness and worried that if she even tried to head that direction that no one would be able to catch up to them in time to save her. Liz was a far better rider than she was. She had to trust to her head start and her horse's speed.

Her hair cleared out of her eyes for a moment and she realized they were headed in the general direction of the mountain Zack had pointed out earlier. The outlaw hideout! If she could make it there she could hide. Hopefully that would give the others enough time to wake up and Zack would figure out where she'd gone.

She tugged the reins slightly to the right and the horse responded, lining himself up with the mountain. She dared not risk trying to look over her shoulder, her balance was too precarious as it was. She just had to pray that Liz was continuing to follow her.

With every step she felt herself jarred to the bone. She tried to adjust to the horse's rhythm and found herself leaning lower and lower forward. It was terrifying, but she felt like part of her was beginning to sing. She felt so alive.

They were closing in on the mountain fast. Zack had said that the cave was just around the side. He hadn't said which side, though. As she approached the base of the mountain she took a chance and urged her horse to the right.

She raced past some trees, hoping they would obscure her from sight so that she could find the cave and get in it without Liz seeing her. The terrain turned rocky and her horse slowed. She pried her left hand off the pommel and pushed the hair out of her eyes as she searched for something that could be a cave entrance.

There! It was beneath a large outcropping of rock. She would have thought it was just a shadow if she hadn't been looking for it. She turned her horse's head and made it into the confines of the cave before pulling him to a halt.

She blinked, trying to let her eyes adjust to the darkness that suddenly surrounded her. Her horse exhaled loudly and pawed at the ground. They had to move farther into the cave so they wouldn't be heard. She tried to urge the animal forward, but he didn't want to go. Finally she dismounted and stepped in front of him. She pulled the reins over his head and held them like she'd seen the cowboys do when they were leading the horses.

She took a couple of cautious steps forward before tugging on the reins. Silver reluctantly started to walk forward.

Without any sort of flashlight it was slow going as she felt her way along, hoping not to bump into any walls or trip over anything. When the last light from the opening of the cave had disappeared she stopped, holding her breath and hoping that they were far enough in that Liz couldn't hear them.

She waited what seemed a lifetime. Finally, there ahead of her, she could see a faint glow. Maybe that was the turn in the cave that would lead to the secret valley.

Suddenly she heard a horse whinny behind them. She placed her hand on her own horse's nose, hoping he wouldn't try to answer. She heard the sound of hoof striking rock.

"I'm going to find you," Liz called out suddenly.

Just be still, she doesn't know we're here, Cindy told herself. *Hopefully she'll just go away in a few minutes.*

Slowly, steadily, though, she heard Liz's horse walking forward into the cave. She gritted her teeth, wondering how close she should let them get before pressing forward.

Silver answered the question for her by letting out a whinny. Cindy winced but began walking the horse forward as quickly as possible. She finally reached the right hand turn and was surprised to discover that wasn't where the wan light was coming from. Instead it seemed to be emanating from a small hole in the ceiling a little farther on. She turned, hoping that Liz would think she had continued on toward the light.

A dozen feet down the branch tunnel she could finally see faint light at the end of it. She pressed on faster, eager to be out of the cave before Liz made it to the turn. She kept going and the light grew stronger until finally she and Silver burst out into a small valley with green grass and a ramshackle cabin on the far side.

Cindy made for the cabin with the horse in tow, unsure of what she would find.

The earth shook beneath Jeremiah and he forced himself awake. He could barely get his eyes open and when he did the world was blurry. He could hear a terrible, crashing sound and it took him a moment to realize it wasn't inside his head.

I've been drugged, he thought as he struggled to get his senses to function. He forced himself up onto his hands and knees and his eyes fell on the half empty water bottle sitting next to his sleeping bag.

He looked around for Cindy but he didn't see her. He shoved Mark hard, but the other man didn't even twitch.

Meantime the roaring was growing louder.

Jeremiah forced himself to his feet and turned around. Less than a mile away there was a cloud of dust that the sound was emanating from.

He blinked in shock as his drugged brain tried to grasp exactly what he was seeing. Moments later he tried to kick the cowboys awake, but it did no good. Everyone had been drugged with the water and the rest had drunk more than he had. There was no way to wake them and warn them about what was happening.

The cattle were stampeding.

He shrugged his hands out of the ropes that were loosely binding them. Then he grabbed Zack's gun from its holster which was right next to the man's pillow. Jeremiah turned, saw a couple of horses nearby still saddled, and ran for them.

He leaped onto the back of a grey horse and kicked the animal toward the cattle. The stampede was just beginning and there was some confusion as some of the cattle continued to mill about.

He had to find a way to stop them or at least turn them otherwise they would run right through the middle of camp trampling all the sleepers to death including Mark and Traci.

As he rode he cast quick glances around searching for Cindy but he didn't see her. Worry flooded him and he hoped she was in a safe place. As he reached the front of the herd he had to force all other thoughts from his mind.

He turned his horse just before the herd crashed into them and raced alongside the leaders. He needed to get them to change course, even if just by a few degrees.

He angled his horse closer into the leader but the cow refused to give ground. Jeremiah pulled out the gun and fired. It worked, the cow veered from the sound, bumping into the one next to it who slowed before also shifting over. He fired again and the herd shifted again slightly. It might be just enough.

Then out of the corner of his eye he saw a big steer break from the pack and head straight for the sleeping men and women. There was no way Jeremiah could cut him off in time and he couldn't risk others following him. He took careful aim, fired two shots, and dropped the beast just as it reached the edge of the camp. It fell hard, just a couple of feet from the first sleeping bag.

He gritted his teeth, watching to see if any others would make a break for it. He dared not slow down, though, lest the cattle behind trample him and his horse. He could feel the animal's terror, but the horse was well trained and was responding to his every command, clearly trusting his rider to get him through this.

Meanwhile Jeremiah was putting absolute faith in the animal. One false step from the horse and they'd both go down to their deaths.

Jeremiah and the rest of the herd raced by, barely missing the camp by a few yards. He kept glancing over his shoulder to make sure that there were no other dangers and he practically held his breath as he watched the river of cattle streaming past.

Once all the cattle seemed to be clear he urged his horse to put on a fresh burst of speed so he could get out in front of the herd. The animal stretched out running at top speed and Jeremiah leaned low over the horse's withers as he urged him onward. Finally, he pulled the horse up short, and spun him around. They were now facing down the herd. The beasts were rushing forward at a frightening speed and he knew he had one chance to get this right. He waited until the leaders were close enough that it would matter and then he fired his remaining two shots.

It worked, the front cattle slowed. Some of the cattle in the back plowed into them and a few went down, but that helped build a barrier between the others and Jeremiah.

A ripple passed backward through the herd as cattle slowed to avoid collision with the ones in front. He held his breath, hoping that what he had done was enough.

All the cattle stopped running at last. They milled around for a couple of minutes before finally settling down. Some even started to nibble at the grass and he just shook his head in amazement. One moment they were a destructive, powerful force of nature and the next they were just cows again. Things could change so quickly it was amazing.

His horse's muscles were twitching and the animal was drenched in sweat. Jeremiah could relate. After a couple of more minutes he turned his horse and headed back for the camp, letting him walk slowly which would help cool him off.

He had nearly reached the camp when a figure detached itself from the others and began walking toward him. He recognized it a minute later as belonging to Zack. The cowboy was coming out to meet him on foot.

When he reached him, Jeremiah pulled his horse to a stop.

Zack reached out and patted the horse on the neck and the animal dipped its head.

The cowboy looked up at him grimly. "Nice job."

“Thanks,” Jeremiah said, handing him his gun back.

Zack reloaded the weapon and then holstered it.

“The horses spooked. I’m going to have to round them all up.”

“Then you’ll be needing him,” Jeremiah said, patting his horse’s neck before dismounting and handing the reins to Zack.

“Much obliged. You know, I don’t believe for a second that you’re guilty. Didn’t think so before, really don’t think so now.”

Jeremiah smiled. “I feel the same way about you.”

“So, are you figuring like I am, that we were drugged.”

“Absolutely.”

The cowboy shook his head. “I’d like to get my hands on whoever did that.”

“I don’t know who was responsible, but I’m pretty sure whatever they used to drug us was in the water.”

Zack shook his head. “That’s pretty low down. Glad I didn’t have a chance to have a second one then.”

“I only had half of my bottle. I think that’s what allowed me to wake up when I heard the commotion. If you had a full bottle, though, how come you’re awake now?” Jeremiah asked.

Zack laughed grimly. “I defy anyone to sleep through that no matter how knocked out they are or by what. That stampede could have woken the dead.”

“So, I take it the others are finally awake?”

“Getting there. Some more than others.”

“Have you seen Cindy?” Jeremiah asked.

Zack thought for a moment and then shook his head. “You know, I can’t say that I have. I’m still pretty out of it, though.”

Fear flooded back through him again. He took a calming breath. Just because Zack couldn't remember seeing her didn't mean that something had happened to her. He would just have to get back to camp and figure out what was going on. For all he knew she could have been in the wagon when everything happened.

Jeremiah heard footsteps and he turned to see who was approaching.

"You killed my partner," Curly snarled.

Curly was holding a gun and it was aimed right at Jeremiah's heart.

19

"Curly, don't be a fool. This man didn't kill anyone. In fact, he just saved all of us," Zack said.

"Put the gun down," Jeremiah said softly, in as soothing a voice as he could manage. He was calculating how long it would take him to grab Zack's gun out of its holster if he had to. Mark's gun which he had borrowed was empty now.

Curly was shaking like a leaf, rage mixing badly with the drugs in his system and together they made him unpredictable and dangerous.

"Settle down, Curly, we can figure all of this out," Zack said.

Jeremiah could tell Curly was beyond reason at that point.

"I'm going to give you one last chance to put that gun down," Zack said, his voice hushed. It got Jeremiah's attention. There was something dangerous in the way he said it. The doctor was getting ready to do something and Jeremiah realized it might be best to let him make his move.

"No, I won't, he kill-"

Zack's hand flashed downward and a moment later there was a boom as he fired his gun. Curly's gun went flying and the cowboy grabbed his hand in agony.

Jeremiah retrieved the gun and reluctantly handed it to Zack. Zack reholstered his own weapon and then tucked Curly's into the gunbelt.

"That was some fast draw," Jeremiah commented.

"When you're the great-great-grandson of a gunfighter it kind of comes naturally. At least, it does in my family," Zack said. He then addressed Curly. "Let's get you back to camp and get that hand bandaged."

All the fight had gone out of Curly and he nodded meekly.

"We can do a headcount there and then worry about rounding up the horses," Zack said to Jeremiah as he handed him back the horse's reins.

Jeremiah nodded, worried about Cindy.

Together the three walked back, Jeremiah leading the horse and Curly still clutching his injured hand.

Back at the camp Wayne and Junior were standing over the dead steer that had nearly killed them, both bleary eyed and in shock. Hank and Mark were both pacing back and forth, clearly trying to wake themselves up. Traci, Norman, and Kyle were all sitting on their sleeping bags with both Traci and Norman swaying slightly. It made sense. Whoever had drugged everyone had done so equally and with the least body mass Traci and Norman should have been the most heavily affected. Of course, this poked serious holes in his theory that Norman was the killer.

Zack headed straight for the wagon, presumably to get his medical kit.

"Where's Cindy?" Jeremiah called anxiously to the others when they got close.

Everyone turned to look at him.

"I don't know, I haven't seen her," Mark said at last as Jeremiah handed him back his gun. The detective took it without comment.

Warning bells went off in Jeremiah's mind. "What about Liz?" he asked, naming the one other person who wasn't present.

"Haven't seen her since dinner," Hank spoke up.

Since dinner. Jeremiah closed his eyes and forced himself to remember dinner, particularly what he could about Cindy and Liz. He could remember feeling drowsier and drowsier as he ate, watching everyone who had been out in the sun and the dust down their water bottles in seconds.

Except for Cindy who hadn't touched hers and Liz who had been drinking some sort of juice instead.

"Liz is the killer," he said. "She tried to drug everyone with the water, but Cindy didn't touch hers."

Norman had turned white as a sheet. "That's a lie," he said through lips that trembled. "Liz would never hurt anyone."

In a moment everything fell into place. He remembered the way Liz had put her hand on Norman's shoulder that second morning when he had discovered the film footage was destroyed and the way he had looked at her. Norman had had a love letter in his pocket and Liz had had a pen and paper in hers. Kyle wasn't Liz's type. Nice, unassuming Norman was his exact opposite. This was supposed to have been Norman's show. The whole thing had been his idea and in the end he wasn't even going to get to be the cinematographer on it.

"You and Liz are a couple," Jeremiah said.

Norman flushed, but nodded.

"And she knew this show was your idea, that it meant everything to you. She knew that it had been taken away from you."

Realization dawned on Norman's face and it was painful to behold the look of horror that crept in.

"She was so angry," he said, sounding stunned. "I'd never seen her like that. I mean, she's always passionate, intense, but that...I told her to let it go, that there was nothing that could be done about it. She told me to have faith; that it would all work out in the end. When they called me to tell me that Martin had had a heart attack and that they needed me to take over, I felt awful. At the same time, though, I thought maybe it was fate, I was supposed to work on the show after all. I thought the universe was making things right."

"But it was actually Liz killing a man to get you on this show," Mark chimed in.

"I never knew."

"But you suspected," Jeremiah guessed from the sudden look of guilt that flashed across his face.

"No, but I should have," he whispered. "When I got here I told her how excited I was to be the cinematographer for the show. She told me that she thought I was going to end up being the host. I just laughed and told her Kyle would never step aside. I never dreamed..."

Zack arrived back from the wagon, his medical bag in his hands and a grim look on his face. "Whoever drugged us raided my bag to do it," he said grimly.

"It was Liz," Traci informed him. "Jeremiah just figured that out."

"So now, the question is, where are she and Cindy?" Mark asked.

"If Cindy figured it out, Liz would be trying to kill her," Jeremiah said. "Cindy must have taken off."

Zack shook his head. “Where? We weren’t out long enough for them to have gotten that far.”

“Not on foot. When I came to and grabbed a horse I didn’t pay much attention to the others, but I know I didn’t see Silver,” Jeremiah said.

“And thanks to the stampede we have no idea how many horses are actually missing,” Zack said.

“Cindy had to be in imminent danger to get on a horse,” Mark muttered.

“She is, and Liz is chasing her,” Jeremiah said. He swung up into the saddle.

“She wouldn’t possibly head for town. It’s too far, she doesn’t know the way, and I don’t see Cindy thinking she can outrace Liz for that long,” Traci said.

“She’d look for someplace to hide,” Jeremiah said.

“I know where she’s heading!” Zack exclaimed. He tossed his medical bag to Mark.

Jeremiah leaned down and grasped the other man’s hand and pulled him up behind him onto the horse. Hopefully along the way they’d find a second mount, but he had no time to waste looking for one now.

“That way,” Zack said, pointing toward one of the nearby mountains.

Jeremiah urged the horse forward and they were soon galloping toward the mountain. “How do you know where she’s heading?” Jeremiah shouted.

“I told her about an outlaw hideout my ancestors used that’s right over there. It’s the perfect place to hide,” Zack shouted back.

Just ahead and to the left Jeremiah spotted a shape moving toward them. It was one of the horses that had scattered because of the stampede, a palomino that he believed was Zack's preferred mount. Jeremiah angled the grey toward the other horse and slowed slightly as Zack emitted a high pitched whistle.

They reached the other horse and the palomino turned and began running next to them. Jeremiah felt Zack tense up and then the cowboy leaped onto the other horse. He slid sideways in the saddle for a moment but then quickly regained his balance. "Good girl, Princess," he heard him shout.

Zack and Princess surged ahead, leading the way, and Jeremiah kept the grey just behind them.

Hold on, Cindy, I'm coming.

The sun was beginning to set and it was casting long shadows across the valley. Cindy had tied Silver's reins to a rickety looking rail on the side porch of the cabin. The stairs creaked as she mounted them and she gazed anxiously at the worn boards on the porch as she crossed it. The door opened with only a little shove and she closed it behind her more out of habit than anything else. The floors inside groaned beneath her weight and everything was coated with a thick layer of dust. She cast her gaze about, searching for anything she could use as a weapon even as she prayed that Liz would get lost in the cave and never make it this far.

She ventured farther in. There were a couple of old chairs, one with dark stains on it that she suspected might be blood. There was an ancient wood burning stove in front of them. She could see a couple of doors on the back wall that she suspected led to bedrooms.

Some rusty, cast iron cookware hung on nails on another wall. She walked over, took down a skillet and hefted it experimentally. It was heavy and she wondered if she hit Liz in the head with it if it would be enough to knock her out. She would think so.

She explored the rest of the cabin, even poking her head into the bedrooms, but didn't find anything that resembled a weapon.

Then she heard the sound she'd been dreading. The stairs outside creaked. She moved swiftly to the side of the door and held her breath, waiting for it to open. Her hands were sweating and she struggled to hold onto the skillet. It had grown very dark in the cabin while she was searching and she hoped she'd be able to find her way back to the camp once she knocked out Liz.

The door flew open, a figure stepped in, and Cindy swung for all she was worth. The skillet bounced off a shoulder before hitting her target's head. There was a grunt before the body hit the ground. She leaped over the legs and ran across the porch and down the steps. She took a half dozen steps toward Silver when something rushed out from behind the horse and tackled her.

Cindy screamed and thrashed on the ground. Hands wrapped around her throat and she kicked out as hard as she could. She tried to jab her fingers upward, aiming for the eyes, but her attacker was moving her head back and forth.

Her head. In a flash she realized that it was Liz on top of her. Who had she hit then in the cabin?

"That's enough!" a stentorian voice shouted.

Cindy twisted her head to the side and in the fading light saw Jeremiah leaping off his horse.

Liz grabbed her hair and hauled her to her feet. Before Cindy could move something cold and sharp pressed against her throat. She realized it was Liz's knife.

She stared at Jeremiah, willing him to tell her what to do.

"It's over, Liz," Jeremiah said, hoping to keep her eyes focused on him. "We know you killed all those people trying to make sure Norman could be the host of the show."

"He deserved it! Do you know how many years he has worked and slaved for an opportunity like this? He comes up with the perfect show, the network loves it, and then they take it away from him! I couldn't just stand by and let that happen."

"So, was Martin an accident or were you trying to hurt Kyle then, too?" Jeremiah asked.

"I was just trying to knock Martin out," she sobbed. "I figured if he was hurt enough they'd bring in Norman."

"And then if you could kill Kyle-"

"I just wanted to hurt him. It should have been him riding that horse, not Cindy."

"And when your plans kept failing you realized you had to up the ante," he said. "You didn't know how much poison to put in his salt because you didn't know how much he would eat and you couldn't risk him just being a little sick."

"And then Brent ruined everything," Liz sobbed. "He hates that stupid truffle salt. Everyone knows that. I never dreamed he'd taste the food after he put it in there."

"But Roddy suspected you."

"Apparently he saw me when I was messing with the salt. He went running off for the doctor and he ran into Tex and told him that Brent had been poisoned and that he thought I'd done it."

"And Tex was working with you?" Jeremiah asked.

"No. He killed Roddy, though, and told me to meet him out past the bathrooms and what time. He rode out supposedly for town and then circled back. I pretended to go to the bathroom and I met him. He wanted to blackmail me. He said I'd never be able to prove that Roddy hadn't just been trampled by the cattle, but that he could prove I killed the others."

"And you stabbed him," Jeremiah filled in.

Liz nodded. "He didn't think I was strong enough to do something like that."

"But you haul that heavy makeup kit all the time in and out of trucks and wagons and you're very strong."

"Very strong," she echoed.

She was losing it, falling apart at the seams. The only question was, when she finally came completely unhinged would she collapse or go berserk?

Cindy was staring intently at him and he could practically read her mind. She wanted to know what she should do. The last time they'd been in a situation even remotely like this he had been armed. He wasn't this time and even though Zack had gotten up and was slowly creeping into position behind Liz he didn't want to risk Cindy's life one moment longer than he had to.

He very slowly, very deliberately lifted his right foot and then stepped down and then moved his right arm pushing the elbow behind him. Liz probably just thought he was fidgeting.

Cindy, though, understood.

She stomped down on Liz's foot and drove her elbow into the other woman's stomach. Then she grabbed the arm with the knife in both hands. She dropped to a crouch, arched her back, and flipped Liz over her shoulder.

Jeremiah rushed forward and snatched the knife up, marveling at what Cindy had just accomplished.

Liz fell apart, sobbing and wailing.

"It's over," Jeremiah told her.

"Nothing is ever over!" she screamed before throwing herself face forward into the dirt.

"Nice swing," Zack said to Cindy a minute later after he had retrieved some rope from his horse. He tied Liz's hands behind her in swift fashion.

"I'm sorry," Cindy said.

"No, you were right to hit first and ask questions later. I'm just glad my shoulder took most of it."

"You're considerably taller than who I was expecting to come through the door," she noted with a faint smile.

Jeremiah felt himself relax slightly. If Cindy was smiling, everything was going to be okay.

Thanks to the flashlights that Zack had in his saddlebags they made it back through the cave. Zack led Liz's horse on a lead rope and Cindy followed behind with Jeremiah bringing up the rear. Once on the other side they were able to ride slowly as the moon rose. Jeremiah told her about the stampede and she was relieved that everyone had made it through okay. She in turn told him the details of what had happened with Liz. It took what seemed like a lifetime but they finally saw the campfire.

Silver broke into a trot, clearly sensing that he was due for a rest when they got there and she let him have his way. Mark and the others hailed their return with relief. She couldn't help but feel sorry for Norman, though, who was in intense distress over what Liz had done for him. It was going to take him a long time to come to terms with it and she resolved to add him to her prayer list. No one deserved to live through the hell he was clearly putting himself through.

He went to bed early. The rest of them sat around the fire, not talking much. After an hour Mark suggested they should get some sleep. Hank agreed. No one moved for another hour after that. Finally one by one everyone headed off to their sleeping bags until only she and Jeremiah were left.

"Thanks for coming after me...again," she said.

"That was clever of you to lead her away from the rest of us."

"It was the only thing I could think to do. She was armed. I wasn't. I had no idea how long the drugs would last but she said hours."

"It probably would have been hours if it hadn't been for the stampede."

"We should go on a real vacation one of these days. One where there's no killers, no bodies, just us."

He chuckled. "Given our luck we'd have to vacation on a private island somewhere."

"That sounds good. Think you could arrange it?" she asked with a smile.

"Probably," he said, giving her an odd look that she couldn't interpret. She decided not to worry about it. Right now they were both alive and well. That was all that really mattered.

20

Righteousness. They had arrived at last. Cindy practically fell off her horse when they pulled up in front of the small hotel. The town was like something between a ghost town and a shrine to the old west as it had been. There were cars, but none of them were allowed on the main street.

They had stopped at a ranch just five miles outside of town where they had met the owner of the cattle drive excursion company and handed the cattle over to him and the sheriff whom they had handed Liz over to. Representatives from the television station were also there to take charge of the equipment.

Originally they were supposed to have spent the night in the bunkhouse at the ranch, ending the trip just as it had started. It had been unanimously decided, though, that the survivors would instead spend the night in the hotel in town which would provide for greater comfort and not conjure up bad memories of that first night.

The tiny hotel had ten rooms and they took all ten of them with only Traci and Mark sharing a room. The rooms were up a creaky flight of stairs that felt like they were original to the building. Cindy just hoped the rooms had been updated to include modern plumbing. She needed a shower badly.

She was in room number seven and when she opened the door she breathed a sigh of relief. The interior of the room retained a certain old fashioned charm but had modern conveniences.

She shut the door, dropped her backpack on the floor, and made a beeline for the shower.

She had to wash her hair three times before it felt truly clean. When she finally exited the shower she dressed in her only pair of clean clothes and headed downstairs.

Jeremiah and Hank were sitting in front of the fireplace in the living room. Jeremiah glanced up at her with a smile and she wondered how he could possibly look as refreshed as he did. The shower had done wonders for her, but she was still sure she had to look beyond exhausted.

"We gave them a bit of a surprise. Dinner won't be ready for another half hour yet."

She nodded even as her stomach began to growl.

"Come sit with us," Hank said, gesturing to an empty chair between them.

She sank gratefully into the cushy plushness of the chair and was embarrassed when a groan of rclief escaped her.

"It sure beats a saddle or the ground," Hank said with a rare smile.

"It certainly does."

The others began to wander in slowly. Mark and Traci both looked sore but much more at peace. Zack looked completely different in khakis and a polo shirt. Curly was wearing a Lone Ranger T-shirt with a clean pair of jeans. Wayne and Junior both looked pale and were moving stiffly. Finally Kyle showed up looking more rested than he had any right to.

"Norman's not going to be joining us for dinner," he announced. "Poor guy feels like he's responsible for his girlfriend going all crazy. I tried to tell him it wasn't his fault, but I couldn't get through."

"Dude's going to need some major therapy," Junior said.

"Lot of guilt to carry around that he doesn't need to," Zack noted.

"When it's your significant other you share everything with them, the good and the bad. Of course he's going to feel terrible for a while," Traci said quietly.

Cindy saw Traci squeeze Mark's hand. She, of all people, would certainly be in a position to understand that.

Jeremiah glanced at his watch. "Still another ten minutes until dinner," he said.

Traci's face lit up. "Perfect! I saw that there was a gift shop in the back. That's just enough time for Cindy and I to go shopping."

Cindy wasn't sure how she'd gotten roped into that, especially when her sore legs would have preferred to stay right where they were. Traci looked so happy, though, that she hauled herself out of the chair and plastered on a smile.

"And I thought we were going to escape this trip without shopping," Mark said with an exaggerated sigh. Cindy could tell, though, that he was pleased that his wife had found something to be excited about so soon after the horror they had lived through.

A minute later Cindy and Traci were inside the hotel's tiny gift shop which was crammed with all kinds of western themed tchotchkes. The first thing Traci grabbed were a dozen postcards showing the surrounding landscapes.

"I didn't get to take any pictures," she explained. "Plus, I want to send a postcard to my sister. We always do that when we travel and she has sent me a lot more than I've gotten to send her."

Cindy nodded even as her eyes were drawn to a little miniature white horse figurine that reminded her of Silver. She picked it up. She really should get a souvenir of this trip, awful as it had been. She took it to the register where she spied a pack of playing cards that she could add to her tiny collection. Pleased, she bought both items and then watched as Traci wandered around the store for another five minutes admiring various things until she, too, was finished shopping. Aside from the postcards she also got a horse figurine, a pen, and a horse suncatcher.

"We should hang out more often," Traci said as they exited the shop.

"I would like that," Cindy said.

"And I promise we don't have to talk about you-know-who if you don't want to."

"It's a deal."

They returned just as the group was being ushered into the dining room. Cindy had to admit it was a relief to sit down on another real chair and she was looking forward to good, hot food that she didn't have to worry might be poisoned.

Apparently she wasn't the only one. When the platters of food came out and were set on the table family style everyone descended on the fried chicken and barbeque ribs as if they were starving.

The whole meal passed largely in silence as the group of tired people expended all their available energy on stuffing themselves. When at last it was over Cindy was sure she wasn't the only one feeling drowsy and content.

One by one the others excused themselves and headed upstairs until only she, Mark, Traci, and Jeremiah remained. The four of them just stared at each other for a moment in silence.

Finally Mark raised his glass of soda. Cindy had noticed that none of them had had water for dinner opting instead for the soda.

"To us. We made it through another one," he said by way of a toast.

"And nobody killed my brother, including me," Cindy said with a wry grin.

They all clinked glasses and drank.

"Apparently they're sending a car for us tomorrow late afternoon that will get us to the airport," Jeremiah said when they had all set their glasses back down. "We'll have several hours to explore the town if we want."

"No offense, but I really just want to get out of here and back home," Mark said.

"I think it will be fun," Traci said with a grin. "The adventure continues, but without any more dead bodies."

"I'm all for that," Cindy said.

The four of them sat and chatted for almost another hour, just decompressing. It felt good, but Cindy was getting really tired and she finally decided it was time to head upstairs.

"I'll head up, too," Traci said.

"I'll be up in a while," Mark told his wife.

The two women headed for the stairs. In the hallway Cindy hesitated. "I think I'm going to check on my brother," she told Traci.

"Okay, I'll see you in the morning."

Cindy knocked on her brother's door and he answered wearing sweats and the same old, overly small Star Wars

T-shirt he had been wearing that first night. He ushered her inside and closed the door.

"I haven't had a chance to say thank you for saving my life," he said without preamble.

"What are sisters for?" she asked.

"Seriously, what you did, what you do? Solving crimes? It's amazing. I think you're my hero."

She didn't know what to say to that. He seemed sincere. "Thanks," she finally said.

He nodded.

She cleared her throat, feeling uncomfortable with not knowing how to respond to that. She stared again at the shirt.

"I keep thinking that T-shirt is familiar," Cindy said.

Kyle looked at her strangely. "It should be."

"Why?"

"It was Lisa's. She was wearing it the morning before she died."

Cindy's heart felt like it was being squeezed to death. "What?" she asked.

He nodded. "I always wear it at the start of every adventure to honor her spirit and at the end of every adventure to remind me to be always be thankful to be alive."

She felt her knees give away and she fell onto a chair. She buried her face in her hands and felt something inside her break loose. She didn't know how long she cried, but when she finally looked up she could tell that Kyle had been too.

"Well, that was...something," she said as she wiped the tears off her cheeks.

"Yeah. Guess we both needed it after everything that's happened the last few days," he said.

Try the last several years, she thought.

She stood slowly. She was beyond tired and the best thing for both of them right now would be to get some rest.

She gave Kyle a hug which he returned. Finally she broke away.

"Now, I want you to look out for yourself. You shouldn't take so many risks, you know. I want to see you again in one piece."

"I'll be careful," he said with a smirk.

She sighed. Some things would never change. Maybe that was for the best.

She turned and headed for the door.

"Oh, and Cind?"

"Yes?" she asked, turning back.

"I really would stay away from Jeremiah. I know that what he and Mark were doing was all a ruse to draw out the real killer, but trust me, there's something not right about him."

"I'll take it under advisement," she said, rolling her eyes.

He crossed the room and grabbed her hand. He looked into her eyes. "I'm being serious. There's something dangerous about him. Trust me, I've played at dangerous things and met some really intense people before and I know what I'm talking about. Whatever it is you don't know about him, I'm pretty sure it's bad. I don't want to see you get hurt."

She was touched by his sincere concern and slightly chilled by his words. "I'll be careful," she said, hoping it would be enough to reassure him.

He shook his head. "Where you're headed, there is no careful."

Before she could ask what he meant the phone rang. He stood for a moment and then with a sigh walked over and answered it. She waved before slipping out of the room and heading for her own.

Jeremiah and Mark had moved back into the living room and settled themselves into chairs in front of the fire after Cindy and Traci went upstairs. He could tell there was something on the detective's mind and he was just waiting for him to say whatever it was.

Mark finally cleared his throat. "Look, a lot of what I said the other day, it was true. I know there's stuff you've done, that you're not all that you appear to be."

"Why are you bringing this up?" Jeremiah asked.

"Because I'm not stupid. Skills like those you possess don't come out of nowhere. There's only a few possible explanations, almost all of them less than savory. The point is, I don't care who you used to be. All I care about is who you are now," Mark said.

The detective stared into the fire for a minute. Jeremiah didn't say anything.

"So, are we good?" Mark finally asked.

"We're good," Jeremiah said.

Mark nodded and stood up. "I'm off to bed."

"Goodnight."

Jeremiah remained by the fire, staring into it and thinking. Mark and he had an uneasy alliance. He just hoped nothing ever happened to disturb it. It was just one more reason, though, why he should go.

He heard the stairs creak and a moment later he could hear someone enter the room. Cindy sat down quietly in the chair that Mark had vacated. She looked like she'd been crying.

"Everything okay?" he asked.

She nodded. "Just working through some old issues, you know?"

More than he could ever tell her. Yet another reason to go.

"Anything I can do?"

She smiled. "You already help more than you could know."

A reason to stay, an inner voice whispered. He knew he shouldn't listen to it as much as he wanted to.

"Just, don't ever die, promise?" she asked.

It was an impossible promise to keep, they both knew that. Still, he nodded. "I promise."

"Good. Now, about those ghost stories we were supposed to be able to tell around the fire."

He groaned.

As it turned out the town of Righteousness was incredibly small, on the cusp of becoming a ghost town. Mark took it all in as he walked down the street. Traci and Cindy were out exploring. Traci had given him the postcard for her sister with strict instructions to mail it. The front desk of the tiny hotel had no stamps but they'd been happy to direct him down the street to the post office. He arrived and went inside.

The inside of the post office was larger than he expected, a sign that the town had likely been far more prosperous at one point. Now it appeared to be run by a single employee who looked older than dirt and certainly appeared in no hurry to do Mark any favors, like selling him a stamp.

As Mark waited for the man to slowly walk up to the counter he took a look around. The place was definitely a bit of a throwback and had seen better days. It was dark and dingy. Faded Wanted posters covered part of one wall and he couldn't help but wonder just how many of those identified in the posters were long since dead.

His eyes landed on one picture. It was grainy and the man was half turned away from the camera. He had dark hair and a thick mustache. Mark stared, dumbstruck. Take away the mustache and there was an uncanny resemblance to Paul. They had the same nose, cheekbones, foreheads. He felt his heart begin to pound in his chest.

"Who is that?" he asked as the old man sidled up to the counter. Mark pointed at the picture, hyper aware that his hand was shaking as he did so.

The old man turned his head slowly, squinting to look at the picture Mark was indicating.

"That there is Matthew Tobias."

He said it as though the name should mean something to Mark, which it didn't.

"What was he wanted for?" Mark asked, finding himself incapable of moving forward to look himself.

"He swindled a bunch of people out of their life savings before skipping town. Let's see, that had to be almost thirty years ago."

"Did he have a family, a son?" Mark asked, licking his lips.

The old man shook his head. "Not that I ever heard tell of, but then again he kept pretty much to himself. Except for the swindling, of course."

Mark clenched his fists at his side. "Where would I find out more about him?" he asked.

"Not rightly sure about that. Most that knew him personal or at least gave him money are dead now. Only ones who aren't moved away years ago."

"I'm going to need a list of names. Anyone you can think of," Mark said.

"What are you, some sort of police officer?"

"Yes, yes I am."

"You seen Tobias?"

Mark shook his head. "Not him, no, but I think I knew someone who was related."

"How can you be sure?"

Because the resemblance was uncanny. More than that, he was in the town of Righteousness and Paul's sister had told Mark that she suspected the boy who claimed to be her brother wasn't when he didn't know the secret password to get into their fort. She had said, though, that what struck her odd was how the boy seemed so agitated on hearing the word. Righteousness. Maybe it wasn't the word itself but the reference to this place that had set fake Paul off when he was trying so hard to pretend to be someone he wasn't.

Was it possible that fate had brought him to the very place he needed to be to learn the truth about his dead partner's identity? It seemed too amazing to be true, but he was looking at a picture of a man who could easily have been Paul's father.

The postmaster gazed at him quizzically, still waiting for an answer.

"I just am sure, that's all," Mark said quietly.

The old man nodded slowly. "I'll do what I can to get you those names."

"I appreciate it."

"Come back in a couple of hours and I'll give you what I've got."

Mark nodded and then turned and left without even bothering to get the stamp for Traci's postcard. The card itself was still clutched in his left hand though he could scarcely feel it.

He found Jeremiah and Cindy with Traci inside the saloon, all of them drinking old fashioned Sarsaparillas.

"What's wrong? You look like you've seen a ghost," Cindy said, her forehead wrinkling in concern as he sat down.

"I think I have," he said.

"You didn't mail my postcard?" Traci asked, sounding more puzzled than annoyed.

He looked down at it then slowly handed it to her. "I'll do it later. I have to go back anyway."

"What happened?" Jeremiah asked.

Mark took a deep breath. "The break I've been waiting for."

Traci caught on instantly. "About Paul?" she asked, leaning forward, eyes fixed on him.

He nodded.

"What does that mean?" Cindy asked.

"It means, that I need help solving this mystery and you two owe me," Mark said, staring first at Cindy then at Jeremiah.

He saw a muscle twitch in the rabbi's cheek and smooth out a moment later. "Just tell us what we can do," he finally said.

Mark nodded as he wondered where on earth they would begin.

Look for

KISS OF REVENGE

The final book in the Kiss Trilogy

Coming October 2013

Debbie Viguié is the New York Times Bestselling author of more than two dozen novels including the *Wicked* series, the *Crusade* series and the *Wolf Springs Chronicles* series co-authored with Nancy Holder. Debbie also writes thrillers including *The Psalm 23 Mysteries,* the *Kiss* trilogy, and the *Witch Hunt* trilogy. When Debbie isn't busy writing she enjoys spending time with her husband, Scott, visiting theme parks. They live in Florida with their cat, Schrödinger.